return *to* KILDARE

MARY A. WASOWSKI

Copyright © 2016 Mary A. Wasowski
Cover Design by Sara Eirew
Editing by Joe Marron
Formatting by JT Formatting

First Edition: April 2016
Library of Congress Cataloging-in-Publication Data

http://authormaryawasowski.com/

Wasowski, Mary A.
Return to Kildare / 1st ed
ISBN-13: 978-0-9969605-3-3

A friend is like a four leaf clover: hard to find, but lucky to have.

–Irish Proverb

This book is dedicated to Aideen McGann, my beautiful friend from Kildare, Ireland. One day, I received a lovely Christmas card from Aideen, and after reading her lovely words, I was inspired and began writing *Return to Kildare*.

I hope one day to visit the beautiful country of Ireland and meet Aideen in person. She has supported my work from the very beginning of my writing journey, and I value the friendship we have found.

NOTE FROM THE AUTHOR

Thank you, readers, for taking the time to read *Return to Kildare*. Please consider leaving an honest review.

Sometimes a story will pop into your head and demand to be heard and written. Most of the time, that's how it works out for me. I could be working on one project and then I have to stop to begin another. *Return to Kildare* was a story that was beckoning me to be told, and I did not stop until I typed "The End."

Instead of one couple defying the odds, in this book there are two: one male and female, the other two males. Both couples are amazing and have their own unique story to tell. In a way, you are getting two stories in one book.

I am passionate with every word I write and invest much of myself into the characters who inspire my stories. We all have known someone who has fought for love and lost it too. In this book, you will experience both.

I hope you enjoy it as much as I loved writing it.

XOXO ...

ONE

War Room

Shaena

Oh, how I loved Mondays! Some would say they hate this day because it was the beginning of a new work week, but not I. Here at Prestige Publishing, it was War Room day.

We all sat at the massive round table that seated all of our best literary agents, pitching new clients and celebrating victories, and I was one of them: Shae Blake, queen of landing the best. I ruled at this house, bringing in the last five best-selling authors from around the world according to *The New York Times, USA Today, and The Wall Street Journal*. Yeah, I was a little conceited, but I worked my ass off for this house and my clients. I got to be part of their journey. There was no greater reward than to see them shine and rise to great heights in their career, and I knew I played a small part in that.

Yes, I was on top, and it was a great place to be. I was a literary agent. I was the best. Today was War Room day, and I had come to play.

"Good morning, sunshine," my partner in crime, Jesse Dempsey, said as he handed me my skinny caramel latte.

"Good morning to you," I replied. "You seem chipper today. Did you get laid last night? Hot guy from the bar? What was his name?"

Rolling his eyes at me, thus confirming what I already suspected, Jesse said, "His name is Roger, and he spent many hours under me last night. So yes, I got laid."

"You are not even trying to hide it. Aren't you a little remorseful that our boss—your former lover—is about to walk in here any minute to see you in all of your post-coital bliss?"

"Not at all. He was the one that would not commit, so fuck him."

I sarcastically responded, "No, thank you, that's your job."

"Not anymore," Jesse smirked as he finished off his drink and tossed his cup in the wastebasket. "Yeah, baby, slam dunk. That makes twice since 8 this morning!"

It was my turn to roll my eyes.

Jesse swung around in his chair to face me and said, "Did you ever wonder why I call you 'sunshine'?"

"My sparkly personality? What else could it be?"

"Try again," he smiled warmly at me.

"Come on, Jess. I have no clue."

"I call you 'sunshine' because you are in desperate need of some sun and, while we're at it, some fun. When was the last time you played Sheet Twister with the opposite sex? Hey, at this point, either gender will work for me as long as he or she makes you less uptight."

Jesse was always blunt and to the point.

"I'm good, Jesse. First off, it's December and I have fair skin, so no tan in my future. Secondly, my work gives me all the satisfaction I need, and besides, I live vicariously through you. Hey, look who's coming in. Your former sunshine just walked through the door. He looks happy...Maybe he got some last night too."

My friend's confident smile now turned to an angry tick of his jaw.

"Whatever, Shae. Shut up and drink your latte."

"Did I hit a nerve of truth? I thought you didn't care about him or who he was dating," I snickered as I took another sip of probably the last latte he would ever bring me.

Judging by the daggers Jesse was shooting toward me, I knew I was right, and it was clear he missed James.

"Give me back that coffee!" he screamed.

"Too late, all gone," I said, as I shook my empty cup at him. I threw it in the wastebasket and screamed, "Slam dunk!"

"Brat."

"Yeah, but I'm your brat."

"For now…until I replace you with a new best friend."

"You wouldn't dare."

"You're right, I won't. I love you too much. Lay off 'my whatever' with James, okay?"

"Okay," I replied as I smiled with a hint of sadness for him.

I reached for Jesse's hand as James entered the conference room. I knew my pal for far too long now. He missed James, that was clear, but they were very stubborn. I tabled it for now and concentrated on why we were here…War Room day!

"Good morning, people. It is going to be a short meeting but an absolutely great day. Before you ask why, let me just say it in two words: Weston James. You can all close your mouths. Believe me when I say I was quite shocked myself when I received his call, and what I am holding in my hand is the invitation that will change our lives. Yes, people, it's a good War Room day!"

James continued, "The reclusive Weston James has requested one of you to pitch Prestige Publishing to be his new representation. He has severed ties with his UK publishing house and agent. Did you feel the walls shake last night?"

"Yeah right, in his dreams," I heard Jesse mutter under his breath.

I elbowed him to be quiet, but of course, James heard and glared over at him.

"As I was saying, last night the literary world was rocked to its core, and it's all because of one man: Weston James. We have been given a gift with a very small window to climb through and leave with a contract in hand. Every agent wants him. Top publishing houses in the UK and the US are having doors slammed in their faces, but not this house. *He* came to *us*, and *I* will do everything in my power to get him under our wing. He came to play, people, so let's get him signed."

I certainly didn't want to sour his mood, but come on! This author was not like most we worked with, or ever dreamed of landing.

I raised my finger, cleared my throat, and said, "James, if I may interrupt."

"Shae, the floor is yours."

"Does anyone else's head hurt right now? Because mine is. People, we are talking about Weston James. His novel, *The Vanishing Raven*, sold nearly 70,000 copies in the first week of publication to become one of the bestselling debuts of all time. You know I love you, James, but how can you be so confident that Prestige can land him when all others have failed?"

Yeah, that earned some shocked looks from the room. Sure, I was the best in the house and cocky about it, but Weston James was a major deal, bigger than any client any of us had ever dealt with.

"You disappoint me, Shae. Where's your faith? I will let you off the hook of doubt. His request makes me confident. As I said, he came to us. I want him in our house like nothing I have ever wanted before."

As my boss said the last words of his sentence, his eyes focused on Jesse, who turned away as if the statement was about them, not our potential new client. I refocused myself and looked again towards James, who had not stopped smiling.

"James, this is an incredible opportunity this house has been given, and I am very happy for you. I apologize for doubting you; maybe it was from the shock. Congratulations to the agent who gets to finally meet the man behind the words."

"Shae?" he said coyly.

"Yes, sir?"

"Congratulations."

"Come again?" I choked out.

Jesse's grin was nearly splitting his cheeks as he laughed at me. Here I was a minute ago feeling sad for my friend. So happy I could entertain him. Jesse was waiting for me to freak out. Jesse knew how much I loved Weston's work. I couldn't help but fangirl over *The Vanishing Raven* when I held the book in my hands for the first time.

"You heard me, Shae. *You* are the one *he* wants to impress him. I have no doubt you will succeed. Everyone give a round of applause to our girl Shae here. I do believe it is going to be a great Christmas, because we have been given the brass ring of literary giants. That concludes today's meeting. If you smell it…Go sell it!"

I was silent as I sat there in the now empty conference room. I was wishing for something stronger than coffee now…like scotch, yeah, that would calm me a bit. Then Jesse walked in.

"Why me?" I asked Jesse.

"Because you are the best, and this freak knows it."

"He's not a freak; he's a genius. I know he is not your choice, but I have followed him since his first novel. His words speak to me as if he was trying to convey a message for only me to understand. Does that sound weird to you?"

"Beyond weird, but I am sure you will love every minute of his weirdness."

"I have to go speak with James."

"Good luck with that. Give him a kiss from me."

"Jesse, just make up with him and put yourself out of this misery."

"I will not. He is the one that will not commit. I was always ready."

"Okay, best friend, I love you."

I gave him a hug and kissed the top of his head. My head was spinning like an out-of-control car. I wished I could help Jesse, but I had enough to handle with the mysterious Weston James.

I grabbed another latte and made my way to James's office. I knocked a couple of times before he called out for me to enter. He was on the phone and gestured for me to sit and wait for him to finish the call. I was fine with putting this off for as long as possible.

I was never nervous about meeting clients. I was beyond confident that I would accomplish even the most impossible task, but something was different about this one. Weston James was a mastermind at his craft. He was young but with an old soul. He lived his life very privately. He had never done a press tour. I had never seen not one single publicity photo, not even on his novels. He did not have any social media accounts. His fans from all over the world had fake accounts where they'd share teasers and photos of muses of his characters.

I finished up with my coffee as James concluded his call. As happy as he appeared in our War Room meeting, he now looked crestfallen. Did Jesse's words affect him on some level where he was feeling regret over their break-up? I knew he heard Jesse on the account of the look on his face. Jesse was my best friend, we pretty much share our lives with the other, and James was not that open, at least not to me. He was all about closing the deal. If only he was that determined in his personal life, then my best friend would be happier. James shuffled some papers around his desk, and then hit a few keys on his laptop before refocusing his attention back over to me.

"I do hope you like Ireland, because you are booked on a flight tomorrow morning," he leaned back and smiled.

I would have choked if I were still drinking my coffee.

"Ireland? Are you serious?"

"Serious like a three-book deal. It does not get any sweeter than that, Shae. In addition, the best part? Prestige does not have to spend a dime. You will be Weston James's guest at his home in Kildare. You will be staying at one of the most luxurious castles—yes, I said castle. I have never been so jealous in my entire career. Don't think for a minute I didn't try to come with, but he only wants you."

My heart skipped a beat. Did he just say Kildare, Ireland?

"James, I'm flattered, but why me? Any number of literary agents in the world, and any publishing house for that matter can pitch him. His departure from his UK house is still up for debate. It shows the rest of us that he does not have any loyalty for the people that have taken him under their wing. I am most certain that his former team worked their collective asses off for him."

"As we will too. Shae, I thought you were the best? You always seem to find a way to tell your coworkers and me every day. You have never shied away from a challenge before, and I will not allow you to begin with Weston James. If I did not believe you were the right person for this job, I would have denied his request."

"Yeah, right…And I don't breathe."

"It's true. This company and stature is everything to me. I have worked very hard at the expense of everything else falling apart in my life to bring Prestige into the same ring with Penguin House, Simon and Schuster, and the world. The business we are in is competitive, but it also drives us to be our best, and you are my best. As I see it, Weston James is staying true to himself. He is beyond a conundrum. It will be up to you to break down his walls to sign him. You have this. Besides, all the time I have known you, you have never taken a single sick day or vacation. As much as this is a business trip, it's Ireland, so go enjoy it."

"Okay, you are seriously scaring me now. Where is James the boss? Because the guy that just gave me that pep talk is an imposter."

He laughed and showed me a half smile.

"He's still here, Shae, but he also knows that he may need to make some changes in his life before work consumes him altogether."

I saw him glance over to a picture on his desk: a group photo of our team, including Jesse, who was standing a bit close to James. He smiled, but then shrugged it off and shut down again.

"Here is your packet. Take the rest of the day off to pack and prepare."

"Thank you, James, I will do my best."

"I know you will."

He went back to his typing, effectively dismissing me. He noticed I was lingering.

He stopped abruptly and questioned, "Is there something else?"

"James, I know this is not any of my business, but the part where I protect my best friend from a broken heart is winning over my choice to remain silent. Do you miss him at all? Because if you are going to tell me no, then I may just have to call bullshit. I really don't want to piss off the boss who just gave me the greatest opportunity of my career, but…you are one of the most honest men I know. Please don't be a liar when it comes to admitting your feelings for Jesse."

He let out a sigh, and rubbed the bridge of his nose.

"You are dangerously close to crossing the line with me, and I would advise you to step back. My relationship with Jesse, for whatever it is, is not your business. You were correct the first time. Please, do both of us a favor, and stay out of it."

"I think you're making a mistake," I said, further angering my boss.

"And that is strike two! Go now before I change my mind and go to Ireland myself."

"Strike two? A sports reference? That's a new one. Fine! I will go, but Jesse is my best friend, and I love him a lot. He would kill me if he knew I was talking to you about him, but call me a silly female who once upon a time believed in the 'happily ever after.' If you were smart, you would not let him go so easily. Ok, now I'm done. Am I fired?" I said, as I held my breath.

"Of course not. I'm sorry for raising my voice with you. If you want the truth, okay, here it is. I don't believe I am ready for what Jesse is expecting from me. He wants a partnership, a marriage, kids down the road, maybe even a dog or two."

I could not help smiling. What James had just said sounded beautiful to me. If I had not become such a workaholic, I could have had all of that by now.

"Have you told him this?"

"In so many words, but they were not anywhere near the conversation that you and I are having now. He got angry, twisted my words, and told me he was done."

"I'm sorry, James. He didn't tell me that."

"Why would he, when it is so easy to blame me for our break-up? I love him, Shae, but I was never one to just jump into the deep end without a life jacket, at least not in my personal life."

"Do you want me to talk to him? If he heard it from me, maybe he would see things differently."

"No, I don't think so. Please concentrate on the task you have been given and not on my love life. I need you to prepare for this meeting. I'm fine, Shae, and Jesse will be too."

"Okay. I'll be in touch. I feel like we should hug now. No? Okay, see you when I return."

I took the packet and made my way out, still not believing this deal was real. I also took a deep breath on how I found my courage to be so blunt with James. I played my "best friend" card today, and thankfully, I still had a job.

As if my day could not get any crazier, my cell phone had not stopped vibrating in my pocket. I ignored it earlier when I was talking to James, but the persistent caller was at it again. I walked into my office, closing the door behind me.

I needed to sit for a minute and process all that happened this morning. When I arrived at work for War Room day, I never imagined my boss telling me he was sending me to Ireland to meet Weston James. I leaned my elbows on my desk and let out another deep sigh.

My nerves were beginning to calm when my assistant knocked on my door to wish me a good trip and to tell me that my mother was waiting on line one. She was the last person I wished to speak with, then I looked to my cell phone, and sure enough, the persistent caller was indeed Charlotte Blake. I aptly named her "Medusa" in my contacts. I shook my head and counted all of the missed calls: nine. What could she want that was so urgent? I guess I could not put her off any longer. I did my usual chant before connecting the call.

"Hello, mother, what can I do for you?" I was not going to be sugary sweet for her benefit.

"You could start by picking up your damn phone when I call you!"

"I have a job. You cannot expect me to drop everything to speak with you the minute you call. What is so urgent that it could not wait until I called you back?" My voice was now higher than I intended it to be.

"Have you checked your day planner recently?"

"My assistant handles my schedule."

"I guess you should fire her then, because she is clearly incompetent."

"Mother, let's leave my assistant out of this, and just tell me why the reason for the call? I have to prepare to go out of town tomorrow, and I must be going."

"Where are you going?"

"Mother, why the call?"

"You tell me first."

"Seriously? It's for work. I have to go, mother. Nice talking with you."

"Shaena Blake, do not hang up on me!" she shouted through the phone.

"Fine! I leave for Ireland tomorrow and will not return for the next week or so. Happy?" I shouted back.

The line had gone silent, and I was not sure if she disconnected our call. I was about to slam the phone down back to its cradle when she began talking again.

"Why are you going to Ireland?" My mother's voice was uncharacteristically low and more subdued.

"As I said, I have work. Now, if you please, tell me why you called, or I really have to go."

"I guess what I have to say is not important anymore."

"You called me nine times. What were you going to say?"

She sighed on the line and reminded me about a charity event in my late father's name. After his fatal heart attack, my mother created a foundation to support heart disease and raise money for awareness. My company always supported the cause, as well as some big names. Anytime I had offered help to be part of it, she would cast me aside because we never agreed on anything. All she wanted was the big names I could bring in and their checkbooks.

"I'm sorry, mother. I forgot that was coming up. I am quite positive that you have everything under control. You always do."

"I did not call to hear your smart mouth, Shaena. Enjoy your trip to…where did you say you were going to in Ireland?"

"I didn't. Why must you know? On the other hand, the better question. Why do you care?"

"I am not the heartless monster you make me out to be. I'm your mother, and I will always have your best interest at heart."

"Your definition of having my best interest is quite different from mine. Who are you kidding, mother? You no longer have any control over my life and the people I choose to have in it. Stop the caring mother routine; it's embarrassing."

"You really feel that way about me after all of this time that has passed?"

"I do. You destroyed me back then, and I could do nothing to stop you, but I can now. Why do we keep doing this? You only call when you want something. You never ask about my job, my anything. I believed we were far apart when I was younger, but after daddy died, we could not be more estranged."

"Why do you hurt me so much? I did my best with you. After your father died, all the responsibility was on me, but do you say thank you? He would roll over in his grave if he could hear you now. Let the past go and move on, Shaena. It will not serve you any good to re-visit any sad memories."

"Sad memories? Mother, that's all I have now because of you.

Thank you for your words of wisdom, but I will live my life on my terms with no help from you. I have to go. Take care of yourself."

Before she could reply, I disconnected the call and left my office with a throbbing headache. She had stopped being a mother to me a long time ago. Why pretend she's all warm and fuzzy now? Charlotte Blake was none of those things. My dad was, to a point, but anytime he would show me any affection, my mother would almost be jealous of it and pick a fight with him.

If only the dreams we imagined at night could be our reality. For reasons I didn't know, or may never understand, she crushed my dreams. She took a part of me that was hopeful and believed that if you had faith, courage, and love in your heart, things would work out the way they were destined to.

She expected me to forget my past. If only it were that easy. She played a starring role in the undoing of my happiness. I was an adult now, and she had no right to ask me anything, especially when it came to my life. I had not easily forgotten, nor would I ever forgive her. Focusing on my education and beginning my career was the driving force to wake up every morning and move forward.

Did she think it was easy to let go of someone who affected my life the way Seamus did? My mother should be happy I was speaking to her at all.

While I was waiting for my elevator, James walked by, surprised to see me.

"Why are you still here?" he said, looking down to his watch.

"As you could see, I'm leaving now."

He nodded with an obvious look of frustration. What changed in the last hour since I left his office? He was so elated earlier. The elevator opened, and I sighed in relief.

What was his problem? He began the day on top of the world, and now he looked like he just got his penis caught in his zipper. I know I overstepped with my questions, but I had to know where his feelings were when it came to Jesse. Stubborn men! He had better figure it out before Jesse gives up on him. He will not wait forever for him to see the error of his ways. They are perfect for each other. This "I'm not ready" crap is for the non-believers like myself. Jesse and James are different; if they pull their heads out of their asses, their dreams will come true.

TWO

I Left My Heart in Kildare

Shaena

Listen to me go on, as if I knew anything about relationships. It was so easy for me to fix my friend's love life, while mine was non-existent. My beloved mother squashed that fairy tale many years ago when she advised me to not believe in love, to guard my heart, and not fall for the ramblings of a young man who didn't know any better. However, Seamus was not like anyone I had ever known. And my mother kept us apart.

My father had moved us from New York to Kildare, Ireland. Our time here was short but probably the best year of my life. I was falling in love with Seamus, and he was falling in love with me.

Wait, I'm getting ahead of myself. We met in secondary school. I was fifteen, and he was eighteen. Seamus O'Toole was the most popular student. He was an athlete but not the typical type. He was on the rowing and track team, a star in both. Giggling girls flocked around him, but he never appeared to be interested in them fawning all over him. He kept to himself on most days…until the day we met.

I was carrying a stack of books taller than me and couldn't see where I was walking. I thought I crashed into a wall, but that wall was actually a broad chest of muscles belonging to one of the most popular boys. I was on my knees surrounded by my schoolbooks and scattered pencils. Tears were threatening to fall when a finger lifted my chin and the brightest blue eyes were looking into mine. His eyes were hypnotizing. His mane of dark red curls fell over the dusting of freckles he had on his forehead. Most redheads had freckles, but his were something else. They were beautiful.

"Houl yer horses, lassie. Where's the fire? Are you alright?" he asked as he replaced his finger on my chin to his hand on my cheek.

I felt a zing of heat rush to the surface of my face. It was a feeling like no other.

When I finally found my voice, he was standing with his hand extended for me to take. Once I was on my feet, feeling embarrassed from my display of clumsiness, I whispered, "Sorry."

"For what? You do not have anything to be sorry for. How do you know I wasn't paying any mind and crashed into you?"

"You are kind, but I do believe it was me."

He smiled and began to pick up my books.

"Stop! I can do that," I interrupted. "I'm sure I have made you late for something more important than this right here."

"Wrong again, lass. I am where I want to be. I'm Seamus O'Toole, and you are?"

My cheeks began to heat once more with just the sound of his voice.

"Shaena Blake."

"That's a lovely name. Nice to meet you, Shaena Blake. Feel free to run into me anytime."

He handed me my books and asked me if I needed any assistance finding my way. I shook my head furiously on account that my voice had gone mute again.

"Okay then. I'll be seeing you around," he said.

And as easily as he appeared, he was gone just as quickly. "My white knight," as I saw him. The days following my less than graceful introduction were boring in comparison. I settled into my classes and blended in with the rest of the crowd. Only for me, I was trying to be invisible. It was easy to do since I had no friends. The girls ignored me, no matter how hard I tried to befriend them. I was an outsider. Mother told me not to fret over it. We would not be here long enough to be missed. My father was more sympathetic to my plight, but in the end, he always agreed with my mother.

One afternoon, instead of going straight home from school, I decided to watch the boys play a game of soccer. It was just a practice game, but still fun to be a spectator in the crowd. Deep down, I was hoping someone would sit beside me and strike up some small talk with me. As I concluded another epic fail of trying to fit in, hope was renewed when he appeared before me. Seamus was smiling and asking if he could join me.

I nearly swallowed my tongue trying to answer him. He looked at me, gave another smile, and dropped his knapsack down to the bleachers.

"We meet again, lassie. What are you doing way up here all by your lonesome?" he asked as his hand touched mine.

Trying not to sound like a complete idiot, I played it off as if what he said did not ring true.

"Well, I'm not alone. You're here with me."

"I certainly am, lass. If I may, a word of advice?"

I lost my confident voice again and gestured to him to go on.

"If you would like to be seen, take my arm and let's give them something they will not soon forget. What do you say?"

I stared into those comforting eyes and found my voice.

I told him, "I'm not sure what you mean. I'm just watching a soccer game."

"Oh, come on, love. You can do better than that. I've been watch-

ing you, and you know what I see."

I was afraid to ask him what I already knew. I was trying so hard to fit in, and god, what I must have looked like to him.

I found my courage and just blurted out my question, "What do you see?"

"I see a beautiful American girl who doesn't know how much she is shining all around us. I cannot say I know how you feel because living in Kildare is all I know, but I have to believe you are lonely living so far away from home. Everyone needs a friend, and if you allow me to, I would like to be your first here in Ireland."

My smile nearly hurt my cheeks, and I took his arm as if it was the most natural thing to do in the world. I felt safe with Seamus, an unexplained feeling I had from the moment we had met. We made our way down the stairs.

Seamus looked over to me and whispered in my ear, "Showtime."

As we reached the last landing of the stands, a group of girls and boys abruptly stopped their conversations, and all eyes were on us. Seamus slowly removed his arm from mine and leaped down to the grass below. He turned quickly and opened his arms for me. Was he really expecting me to leap as he did? Seamus could miss, and my fall would only embarrass me more.

He must have seen my fear, and that's when he said, "Trust me, Shaena. I will catch you."

He called me by my name, and why did it feel so amazing hearing him say it? After another beat, and swooning over his Irish accent, all doubt was gone. I flung myself into his arms, and Seamus caught me flawlessly. He twirled me around gracefully and gently set me down, kissing my forehead.

"Shall we? We do not want to be late for our date now, do we, Shaena?"

No words...absolute silence.

"That's what I thought you would say," he said in front of everyone. "Let's go."

Taking my hand in his, we walked away from the group of on-lookers and walked straight through until we reached the parking lot. I finally caught my breath and leaned against his car.

"Thank you, I think, but I'm not sure why you would do that for me. I hardly know you."

"You know me. Once two strangers collide into each other, it's a known fact that you instantly become friends, or you will have seven years of bad luck."

"I think that relates to broken mirrors," I said as I smiled, knowing I was blushing.

"That may be true, but these days I seem to be breaking the rules, so just go with it."

"Rules?" I asked as I raised my eyebrows in question.

Seamus had not stopped smiling since he had taken me in his arms.

"Yes, rules. Rules that I am now breaking because I'm fiercely drawn to you, and I am going against the socially acceptable way a high schooler is supposed to be. Teenagers are pretty much the same, no matter where you live. You have cliques everywhere, and I'm sure where you're from, seniors are not supposed to be in the company of a freshman. Am I close?"

"You hit the nail right on the head. Although I never had a problem making friends before until I came here. They treat me like a social outcast."

"You intrigue them, as well as me, for that matter. I cannot seem to think of one logical reason why I should stay away from you. I've argued against my desire to know you better, and I've lost every round. So, my beautiful Shaena, I'm here, and I do not care who sees us, hears us, or disagrees with us."

Beautiful? He said I was beautiful. When I looked in his eyes, I easily trusted what I saw and felt. What would it hurt to take a chance with Seamus? I decided to trust my heart and believe him.

"I could not agree with you more, Seamus. Screw the high school

rules of social order. We are not doing anything wrong by talking with one another. It is not wrong to take a walk with each other. And not wrong, but so right that it's perfectly acceptable to catch me in your arms when I jump off the field's bleachers."

"Now that is settled, if you allow me to take you home, I would be most pleased to do so."

"You may, Seamus. Thank you."

"Pleasure is all mine."

I sighed happily, as Seamus took my hand into his and opened up the passenger door for me. If this was a dream, please...no one wake me up.

"Hey, sleepyhead, nap time is over."

I slowly opened my eyes to find Jesse standing over me. We had each other's keys to our apartments, so this was not anything new for Jesse to drop on by.

"What time is it?"

I was still a little sleepy and thankful to my best friend for knowing me so well. He had brought me my favorite latte. With two earlier today, I was surprised I was so tired. Thoughts of Seamus were consuming me, while I should be concentrating on my trip to meet Weston James.

I gave my body a deep stretch before taking my coffee from Jesse. He smiled brightly at me as he waited patiently for me to sit up. I felt as if my body had been run over by a truck. My mind was still in a tailspin of overactive thoughts of my time spent in Ireland. I never allowed myself to go back there in my memories, because it was too painful on my heart. I could thank my mother for that.

"Jesse, have I told you lately how much I love you?"

"Not in the last few hours, but by all means, go right ahead."

He laughed and smiled, showing me his gorgeous teeth. Jesse had light all around him. It was something I had, once upon a time. As long as I had Jesse in my life, all was right in my world.

"What's going on, best friend? Your phone is shut-off, the drapes are closed, and I find you here in a deep slumber when we both know you should be packing for your trip. I was surprised to find you had already left work for the day, and that's when I heard Charlotte had called you. She's always a breath of sunshine."

To hear her name again nearly sent me over the edge. Tears were threatening to fall as I tried to hold them back, setting off alarms with Jesse.

"Talk to me, Shae. What is going on? In all the time I have known you, I never once witnessed you cry or been in this depressing state. You have had unpleasant calls with your mother before, so I am sure you handled her perfectly. For the last time, talk to me. You have five seconds to spill it."

I wiped my tears and placed my coffee down on the table. I got up from my bed and walked over to the windows to let some light in, but too late, it was already night. I lost the entire day daydreaming about Seamus and the future I was supposed to have with him back in Ireland. As I stared down to the city below, I took a few deep breaths and began talking.

"Career-wise, this is an amazing opportunity for me, but my feelings of hesitation are personal. Jesse, what would you say if I told you that I already had taken the trip of a lifetime—a time in my life that I allowed to slip through my fingers and dismissed it as if it never even happened?"

Already up and behind me, he wrapped his arms around my body and held me, speaking softly in my ear.

"I would say that this trip is your do-over, and whatever you let go then, you now have a chance to get back. Am I close?"

"You are, but I'm not sure it is possible."

"Sure it is. Anything is possible. It surprises me after all this time that you don't know that. You can achieve anything you set your mind to. I've seen it, Shae."

"Jesse, I'm not talking about work and all the amazing clients I

20

bring to Prestige. This goes way beyond work. This is personal. I cannot go to Ireland, not even for Weston James."

He let me go and turned me around so I could look at him. My tears were hopelessly falling. I needed to feel this pain, even for a little while. It was better than not feeling anything at all.

"What is this? Come on, Shae, talk to me. What has you so spooked about going to Kildare? Shae, James will lose his shit if you are not on the plane in the morning. You are the only one that can land Weston as a client, and the freak requested you. This is the golden apple, girlfriend. I get this guy is a big mystery, but he must have something really big to debut if he has finally decided to come out from the shadows and reveal his identity to the world, beginning with you."

"I am not afraid of meeting Weston James; he actually has nothing to do with my apprehension and hesitation of going to Ireland. Like I said, it's personal."

"Well, make it professional because this is your job, and if you refuse, James will make sure you don't have one to return to. Come on, drink up, and let's get you packed."

"Jesse, I can't."

"You can, and you will. Stop fucking around, Shae. This damsel in distress is not you at all, so show me your girl balls and let's get you packed."

"Thanks for nothing, best friend. You can leave your key on the table as you get out of my apartment."

"Oh hell no! Do not get your bitch on with me. The sulky child routine may work with your mother, but it will not on me. Grow up! I'm trying to help you before you self-destruct before my very eyes and singlehandedly sabotage your career."

"Fine! Let me help you, too. Why are you so willing to give up on James when we both know you miss him?"

"I'm not doing this with you right now. I'm trying to get your head back in the game, so let's concentrate on work."

"No. Five seconds ago, I was telling you something personal, so work can wait."

"No, it will not. I love you, Shae, but you do not know anything about my relationship with James, not the real one that we have kept private for longer than we both wanted to. It's complicated, and I just cannot share it all with you now. I am asking you not to push me on this and just respect my wishes. More importantly, respect me."

"Fine, when you put it that way."

"Good. Now get your ass in your fucking fantastic walk-in closet, and let's get you packed."

I dropped my head in defeat and followed Jesse into my closet, feeling like shit for my behavior. It was not his fault, and I had no right to take it out on him. Jesse had already begun pulling out blouses, slacks, skirts, and my shoes to match up with all he had chosen. He was silent and not looking at me. We rarely argued, and if I knew my guy, he was waiting for an apology.

He had his share of problems with himself, choosing to walk away from James because he would not commit to him. What a fucking fool! Jesse was the complete package, and James was making the biggest mistake of his life not realizing what he had and could have with Jesse. If only James would just let go of his fears and try making it work. To hell with what anyone thought; this was his life with Jesse, and no one else should matter.

If I was not so afraid back then, I should have acted on my own advice when it came to having a life with Seamus and tell my mother to fuck off, but I was only fifteen and had no choice but to adhere to her every command.

"Jesse, please stop packing for a minute. I'm sorry."

"And what are you sorry for?" he continued and kept his back to me.

"Seriously? You just can't accept my apology as-is? I have to give you a play-by-play of how much of a bitch I was?"

"Yes, you do."

"I'm sorry, best friend. I love you. Thank you for always being there for me even when I try to push you away."

His shoulders slumped forward, and I knew I was forgiven.

"I love you, too," he said before scooping me up in his arms and bear hugging me. "Now, for the last time, what has you so upset about returning to Ireland?"

"It's a long story, and one I don't think I have the energy to tell you about now. You're not the only one with a complicated history with the one you love. We all have a past Jesse. A big part of mine is back in Ireland, and I haven't ever allowed myself to open my heart to that part of my life. I left it behind, because I was so foolish in my thinking."

"I'm dying here! You can't just leave me hanging. Spill it!"

"You're not going to let this go now, are you?"

"No, not when I know how much it's affecting you and compromising your judgment."

"You don't play fair. You owe me a story, too."

"You will get it, Shae, but not now. I think you need more help than I do at the moment."

"Okay, the whole story in two minutes. Start the clock."

"Go!" he screamed as he dragged me over to the couch so I could explain.

"Once upon a time, a shy American girl at the age of fifteen met an Irish boy who she simply fell hopelessly in love with and never got over. He was a few years older than she was, but their differences in age did not matter. Their love was magical—a fairy tale, if you could believe—and then one day, her dreams were crushed when she was forced to leave him."

I continued, "They knew what they had was real, but a stronger force in the girl's life crushed her heart by making her promise to forget Kildare and the boy who captured her heart. Love was for fools, she said. In addition, the girl foolishly believed this, and although she promised the boy she would return someday to be with him, she lied and never looked back. Until today, when her boss told her she was going back to the one place that still held her heart. She was going back to Kildare, whether she liked it or not."

"Come here," he said, as he crooked his finger, and I snuggled into his arms.

Jesse held me as I cried. Where was this coming from? My mother would be mortified if she could see me now, but I tried hard to have little interaction with her. We never got along, and she never tried to see my points of view on any subject we argued over.

"I'm sorry, Shae. Do you want me to come with you? I can make up some excuse with James and take some time off. I can max out my credit cards, and no one has to know. I will be your wingman. Come on, Shae. This is not a movie that we drink wine and eat popcorn over; this is your life. Aren't you a bit curious to at least know what happened to that Irish boy?"

"I appreciate it, best friend, but who knows if he's even there? He's probably married by now, or happily, the free spirit I always knew him to be. I would not want to be the homewrecker in any story, least of all his. Today was the first time in a long while that I allowed myself to really remember what I had lost. I guess talking to my mother did not help either. I have been angry for so long now that it is hard separating the good feelings from the bad ones. I have spent today daydreaming about my past. The memories are flooding back to me after a long time of keeping them buried. I will be fine, I promise."

"If you need me, you know I will be on the first plane to Ireland. You know that, right?"

"I do, and I love you. Can you promise me something while I am away?"

"You know I will."

"Try talking with James, please. He may just surprise you. Say you will try, and I will shut up about it."

"Okay, I'll try."

I wiped my tears and traded my coffee for wine. Jesse ordered take-out, and after he packed my entire luggage, we ate dinner over lighter conversation. After finishing two bottles, I was way past drunk. He tucked me in and kissed my forehead. Before I was completely out, I thought I heard him whisper, "Go find your heart in Kildare," and then my door quietly closed and I was dreaming of exactly that.

THREE

Facing My Past

Shaena

"**A**nother glass of champagne for you?" the first class attendant asked, tending to my needs as if I were royalty.

I politely declined. One glass would be enough to calm my nerves. I needed to be of clear mind when I met with Weston James. I spent the last few hours of my flight analyzing every detail of my pitch speech. I was still reeling from the fact that I was the one chosen to establish a new relationship with this man when many before me had failed.

No expense was spared. When I checked in, a flight attendant escorted me to my first class seat. My expression spoke volumes when the flight attendant smiled behind her laughter. Another request by him. Once I sat down in my seat, the pampering began. This was unreal. I had to text Jesse before we took off. I hesitated calling him, because I knew he would shrill on the line when I told him about my very attentive accommodations.

Of course, he did not believe me, so I snapped a selfie when no one was looking. Flying first class was not uncommon for me to do, but having *the* Weston James's all-out primp service was over the top.

Jesse's reply was too many emoji's followed up by three "OMG's" in all caps. I silently laughed and stowed my phone in my purse. I loved my best friend, and was thankful he accepted my apology.

The captain announced to fasten our seat belts as we prepared to make our final descent into Dublin. I closed my eyes and prayed that I would successfully accomplish what my boss believed I could. If he only knew that work was the last thing on my mind.

I stepped off the plane to see a man holding up a white sign with my name on it. I assumed he was my driver to bring me to Weston James. He was older, but I would guess early fifties. His hair was a dark brown with specks of white that made him look distinguished. It was cut very short and styled in a modern cut. Wearing a three-piece pinstriped grey suit, he looked more like a model posing for a *GQ* issue. He could do any number of things for the mystery writer and picking me up was just a favor. I guess I would find out soon enough. As I approached, I could not help but to observe him a little closer.

His features were strong. Expression was serious, and honestly, a bit intimidating. What was I thinking coming back here? I was nervous to the point that my palms were sweaty. I brushed my hands down my blazer and slacks, as if the wrinkles would magically disappear from the seven-hour flight I just endured. I checked my appearance quickly before exiting the plane. I hoped that I looked presentable enough. When I reached him, he greeted me with a formal pleasantry and took my carry-on bag from my shoulder.

"Welcome back to Ireland, Ms. Blake." he said.

Back? How did he know this was not my first time here?

"Thank you, Mr....?"

"The name is Connor Browne. I work for Weston James. Any request made should be filtered through me. I am available 24/7. Here is my card with my mobile number."

"Pleasure to meet you, Connor, and thank you."

"Shall we go? We are on a tight schedule, and Mr. James does not like to be kept waiting."

"Lead the way."

He nodded and walked slightly ahead of me at a faster pace than I could keep up in my heels. He was icy with me, and I was not sure as to why. When I finally caught up to him, my bags were already in the car, and he was standing with my door open. I gave him the same nod he gave me, and I stepped into the car for the hour-long drive. The divider was up, which was fine by me. Not sure as to why I was receiving this chilly reception, but it also prepared me for my meeting with Weston. If his assistant behaved this way, I could only imagine how he would be.

From what I knew of him, he was simply a very private man. He was thirty years old; however, his month and birth date had not been verified for the public. He never married and had no children to speak of. He owned property throughout Kildare, but it was still unknown if he was truly of Irish descent, or did he choose this country to be a famous recluse?

I was working on very little sleep from the night before, and my eyes slowly began to close. As soon as I was in a deep slumber, his beautiful face came into focus. My Seamus.

I was taken back to the afternoon when we shared our first kiss. It was a chaste one, to say the least, but filled with so much gentility and passion. I came to life when his lips touched mine for the first time.

We skipped classes and took an adventure of our own. His rebellious side intrigued me. Seamus was carefree with no inhibitions at all. He did not care what people thought of him, and although he kept to himself on most days, he had girls following him around like puppy dogs. He was charismatic. It was no wonder why the girls fell at his feet. Why did he want me? He was older by three years, which made a huge difference in teen years. What could I offer Seamus? As if he could read my thoughts, he squeezed my hand tighter, smiled down to me, and washed away all my doubts.

We visited the Ballindoolin House and Gardens. I had never seen anything so beautiful in my life. We took a tour of the grounds as Seamus pointed out all the history of this magical place. We walked through a maze of structured walls of flowers. My back pressed up against a wall of flowers. We were on our own, and this was where he kissed me. He cupped my face and leaned in to give me what no other boy had ever done. I felt wanted, special, and even desired. I had watched enough romance movies to know what that meant, but to experience an unknown feeling with Seamus was not anything I could ever get from a book or a movie. This was beyond imagination, and this was real.

I was not alone in my feelings. I knew he felt the same connection I was experiencing. I did not have to wait long for Seamus to confirm what I already knew to be true. It was his words next that made me believe in the fairy tale I was sharing with him.

"Were you sent to me? It feels like I have been waiting for you, and now you are here with me. I want to show you all of me, as I want to know all of you. Will you allow me, Shaena, to do that?"

His lips touched mine once again as I whispered my breathy reply.

"Yes, Seamus, you may know all of me."

His gorgeous sapphire blue eyes closed for only a minute while Seamus shyly smiled.

"Good answer, lassie, because that's exactly what I intend to do."

Our hands linked, and we continued to walk through the luscious gardens. My legs were at the point of shaking as the surge of excitement heated my blood.

I wish I could shout out what I was feeling, but fearing he might not want that, I kept all of my feelings contained to myself. As if, I could even explain it. I wish I had a friend to talk to. I had not made any new ones here. For now, I had all I needed in the arms of Seamus O'Toole.

Our family traveled so much for my father's work, so establishing friendships was hard to do. My father worked more hours than I could count. I hardly saw him. When he wasn't working, he played golf at the country club, or my parents entertained their friends. I was always sent to my room to be alone with my thoughts, until Seamus came into my life. He understood what I would try to say even before the words passed over my lips. We were friends first and then became something more that only we understood.

With his popularity in school, you would have guessed that Seamus had hundreds of friends, but he did not. He preferred to be alone, but not an outcast. He excelled in school. He was the rowing captain and brought our school the victory cup. When he was not front and center, he was on the sidelines with me, which he told me repeatedly that's where he wanted to be. Taking a walk with me through a garden or just talking was enough for him. Oh, the simplicities of a beginning courtship.

I was completely lost in my dreams of happier times that I did not feel the car stop moving until my door was jerked open and the sunlight blinded me.

"We're here, Ms. Blake," Connor curtly announced.

Already my patience was wearing thin with this guy. I know I was here to woo Weston James, but that did not mean I had to be a doormat to his assistant. What was his problem?

I stepped out from the car as my eyes adjusted to the light. I put on my sunglasses so I could take in the beautiful castle in front of me, one of Ireland's finest hotels. The Barberstown Castle was where I would be staying for the next seven days with Weston James. It truly did not get any more surreal than this. Why this place? He didn't live here, but this was where he requested to have our meeting.

"Shall we go in, Ms. Blake, or will you continue to gawk for the rest of the day?"

"Excuse me? Mr. Browne, I am not sure why you feel it is acceptable to speak to me in the manner you have since we met in Dublin, but I assure you, it is not welcomed by me. If you please, curb your obvious animosity toward me for the remainder of my visit here. I was invited, remember?"

"I certainly do, and I have been so advised. Please, if you will, follow me."

Not giving him the satisfaction, I quickly took my rolling suitcase and shoulder tote from him. He raised his eyebrows at me with a look of surprise.

"Yeah, buddy, I'm a New Yorker, and I am fully capable of carrying my own damn bag without the help from a stuffy, stick-up-his-ass, glorified butler, driver, or whatever your duties are."

He smirked and remained quiet as I followed him inside when greeted by more staff. A kind looking woman introduced herself as Aideen. She was impeccably dressed in a black pencil length skirt with a white blouse and pressed jacket. She looked polished and efficient. Not knowing what her role or relationship was here, I just politely smiled until introductions were made.

"Welcome, Ms. Blake, I am Aideen McGann, and I am the concierge for the Barberstown Castle. I work closely with the owner, and I will be here at your service for the duration of your stay. Please feel free to call upon me for anything you might need or want."

I looked over to Connor, who was still scowling at me but remained quiet. He must have noticed the lingering question I wanted to ask, so he spoke first.

"*I* work for Mr. James, and Ms. McGann works for the hotel."

"Okay then. Thank you for clearing that up for me."

The welcoming Ms. McGann insisted I call her Aideen. Her smile calmed me. She was the complete opposite of Connor. She signaled over to the waiting staff to collect my things and bring them up to my quarters. I was out of my element here and not sure as to what to do next.

"Ms. Blake, how would you like me to address you?" Aideen asked.

"Shae would be fine, thank you for asking."

"My pleasure, Shae. Would you please join me for a cup of tea before you go to your room? I am quite sure you must be weary from your long trip."

"Tea would be lovely, Aideen, and thank you for making me feel welcomed here."

"Of course, you are our guest. Follow me."

I could not help but flash a look of victory toward Connor, the smug bastard. I walked side by side with Aideen as we made our way to a private dining room. The fire was roaring with flickering flames that warmed the room. I sat in a comfortable winged back chair in front of the floor-to-ceiling fireplace to warm my body. I was not sure if I was cold from Connor's reception or the chilly Ireland weather. I was presented with tea and the most delicious blueberry scone I had ever tasted in my life.

"Thank you, Aideen. Have you been in your position here long? It must be very exciting with the long list of guests that travel here throughout the year," I asked as I sipped my tea.

"You've done your homework. Yes, it is very exciting and fast paced. Although you are correct with your knowledge of the castle, your time here will be private with no interruption. The owner has all reservations on hold until business with you is concluded."

She quickly sipped her tea. Is that why it was so quiet here today? Did she mean to tell me that? I shrugged it off and continued our conversation.

"Wow, I didn't know that. Does that happen often?"

"Not really, but this is a special occasion."

Another slip? On the other hand, was Aideen trying to tell me something? If not, she recovered quickly by her easy way of avoidance. My body language usually gave me away, and when I was suspicious of someone or something, it showed.

"As I was saying earlier," she continued, "I have worked here for many years now, having just celebrated my twentieth anniversary. I was not always in a managerial position, but I am now, and I truly love it. I get to live here in a private guesthouse on the property. My position allows me many privileges."

I listened quietly as Aideen went on, but I was not a hundred percent sure she was supposed to share so much with me. Aideen could just be kind, and making small talk comes easily for her.

The castle and surrounding property was stunning and well equipped to entertain many guests here. As I looked around, I could not imagine all this luxury just for myself. I finished my tea and engaged in conversation with her.

"That's amazing. I live in New York, city to millions of people, and I rarely get the opportunity to sit in front of a fire and drink tea. My life is fast paced with no leisure in between."

"Well, I shall hope you take time to explore the grounds while you stay with us, and appreciate all Ireland has to offer. It is an experience you will probably never be able to get anywhere else in the world."

"I will promise to try. My visit here is for work, which I must be getting on with."

"Not today, Shae. You will not be meeting with Mr. James until tomorrow, which leaves today just for you."

She completely took me by surprise with her knowledge to why I was here. My expression must have said it all, because she smiled again with a touch of laughter. Had Connor gotten it wrong? He did say that Weston did not like to be kept waiting. My head was already beginning to throb.

"Don't be alarmed. It was my suggestion for you to take some time after the long trip. Mr. James and I worked closely together to meet all of your accommodations while you stay here at the castle. I assure you, you will have your privacy. We have placed you in a private guest wing of your very own. It is well equipped with a full staff for anything you might need. Mr. James is also residing here and will meet you in the morning, per his instructions."

"You've actually met him?" I asked with curiosity. Of course, she knew him, she just finished telling me so, but the question was off my tongue before I could stop myself for asking.

"Yes, Shae, I have. He is not as scary as you may think; he is just private. From what I know of Mr. James, he takes much pride in his work. He does not wish to be in the limelight, as many of his peers seem to be in. I think he thrives on the mystery. Keep the world guessing. You know what I mean?"

"I do actually. Which is why I have been confused from the very beginning as to why he would request me to meet him."

"I guess time will tell, and hopefully you shall get all of your questions answered. Now, please follow me. You must be exhausted. I will have a bath drawn for you and your things unpacked. Feel free to take a nap or a walk around the grounds. Dinner will be brought to you whenever you are ready."

"Thank you so much. I could use a nap, and soaking in a hot bath would be perfect."

Aideen delivered on everything she offered. I entered the palatial master suite with a hot bath waiting for me. The en suite was larger than my entire apartment back in New York. Flickering candles were all around the enormous sunken in tub. Smells of berries filled the room. I wasted no time at all and stripped down to step in the mound of bubbles that awaited me. I was in heaven and finally allowed myself to enjoy the relaxation my body was now feeling.

I had to stop myself several times from dozing off and drowning, I was so relaxed. My tight muscles now felt like mush. This was just what I needed after my flight and the glacial time spent with Connor.

I remained in the bath until the water turned cold. My fingers were shriveled up and my toes too. I loved it though. After drying my body with a warm towel, I combed out my long dark tresses and put on the thick comfortable robe that was hanging on the back of the door. The fire had been lit in my room, and my eyes did not miss the tray filled with fresh pastries, a pot of tea, and one single stemmed rose. It was a lavender rose.

For a brief moment, my heart began to beat faster as I closed my eyes, remembering another time with Seamus.

"Why the lavender rose?" I asked him.

"Why not?"

"You always give me a purple one, which I love, by the way. I guess I just wondered the reason behind your kind gesture."

"Don't you know, love? I would think it would be obvious by now. You do love the written word from a time now lost to many."

"If you are referring to my taste of books, then I am offended, Seamus. I love English Literature, and maybe I am a fool to believe, but I can't seem to help myself."

I started to have tears in my eyes and could do nothing to stop them from falling. I probably ruined everything with Seamus by asking my stupid question. I felt embarrassed, only proving my mother's opinion of me. I felt foolish. He lifted my chin and wiped away the tears that spilled down my cheeks.

"Oh, you beautiful girl! You are not foolish by any sense of the word. I love that you are passionate and the literary classics fuel your spirit. I give you purple because it is what I feel all the times my eyes find yours."

"How? I just don't understand what you see in me. I am not like any girl who attends our school. My skin is nearly porcelain white. My hair is dark as coal. I am a complete stand out, and not in a good way."

I put my head down once again only to have Seamus lift my chin and lean in to kiss me. He wrapped his strong arms around my body and whispered something that held the power to dismiss all of my fears and insecurities I had so bluntly showed him.

"Love. I love you Shaena Blake. I give you a purple rose because it represents what I have felt for you from the moment I crashed into you. It was love at first sight, and you are my first, and I am hoping you will be my last." He held my hands to his lips as he continued to

place gentle kisses down on them. I was speechless, having been stunned into silence by his own admission. Seamus has just declared his love for me, and all I could do is let more tears fall but only now, they were happy ones.

I smiled and finally looked up at him. He was taller than my small five foot five frame. He was strong, where I was petite. I loved the feeling that I felt when he held me. He was waiting patiently for my reply. I rested my cheek on his chest and gave him exactly what he wanted to hear.

"I love you, too. I have from our beginning, and I shall hope what we feel at this moment will never end. Thank you for loving me, Seamus. You are the first one who ever has."

I made the mistake of sharing my bliss with my mother, who I believed would be happy for me. But I was wrong. She would not allow me to retreat to my room until I listened to what would be another long drawn out lecture.

"Oh, my silly girl! Stop your foolish thinking and forget about him. Why do you continue to allow yourself to believe this boy has fallen madly in love with you?" mother said, chastising me from her vanity table. She was having her hair brushed by her maid, who looked over at me with sadness.

She went on, "You are only fifteen years old. You are young, too young and naive to believe in love. I am sure he is a nice boy, but you need to be smart about this, Shaena. We have been over this more times than I care to remind you. What would he want with you?"

"Mother, I am not foolish. I wish you would have faith in me. Seamus does not treat me like a little girl. He treats me like a young woman with an intelligent mind."

"Sure he does, my daughter, until he whispers all the sweet nothings in your ear and then inevitably takes advantage of you."

"It's not like that, mother! Where do you come up with these crazy delusions? He has been respectful, kind, and sweet. He has only kissed me a couple of times to the point I nearly lost my balance. You should

hear the poetry he reads to me. He wants to be a writer someday. You never know, mother…he could be one of the greats."

She turned around forcibly and nearly knocked over Faith, who was styling her hair. Grabbing the brush from Faith's hand, she hurled it across the room and hit me on my head.

She threatened, "You listen to me, and you listen with both ears and not with your dreamy heart. Love is for fools. I will not sit here and listen to this nonsense any longer. We will be leaving Kildare soon enough and you will eventually forget about Seamus O'Toole. I did not raise my daughter to be lovesick over a boy that will surely break her heart in the end. Stop romanticizing, and grow up! You need to finish school and then on to college. Those two things are your priority; not some boy. Do I make myself clear?"

I was crying inconsolably. I hated her at that moment.

"Stop that crying, right now!" she yelled. "I will make sure for the remainder of our time here in Kildare; you will not leave this house."

"Why, mother? Do you not understand how strong love is? Who hurt you to make you not trust your heart? To not trust love? I see the way daddy looks at you. He loves you, don't you know that?"

My mother hated weakness. I tried to cease my tears, but her words hurt me, and no matter how hard I tried, they kept falling.

"Shaena, I will not discuss my marriage with you. My reasons are mine, and they are not up for debate. I am your mother and will always have your best interest at heart, whether you agree with me or not. I know I sound cold, but you need a firm hand. You are spoiled, and your head is in the clouds. We are going back to the United States, and when we do, you will be enrolled in private school. You need discipline. The Waverly School will provide all you will need to secure your future and get you back on track. Now, I have grown tired of this conversation with you. Let us not discuss this again."

She dismissed me and turned back to the mirror to continue having her hair done. Another night mother and daddy entertained with my father's work friends while I was alone. She put on airs for people who she deemed important and socially suited for her company. I was her daughter. Why didn't I matter to her? A bump was forming on the side of my head, and my tears kept falling as I walked out from her bedroom.

I crossed my arms over my chest and hugged myself. With the dam breached, my tears were flowing. God, she was cruel. I never wanted to leave Ireland, nor did I want to leave Seamus.

After that night, mother kept a closer eye on me. She had a driver pick me up from school and take me straight home. I was seeing less and less of Seamus all due to my mother's interference. I made every effort to see as much of him as I could during school hours, but he had different classes and then his afterschool sports. I counted down to the times when he would have a rowing match at school where I could watch and cheer him on from the stands.

Our stolen moments together were short, but cherished. He said he understood but was not happy about it. He told me that there were other ways of communicating with each other. He would write me letters and have one of his teammates hand it to me. He did not trust I would receive them if mailed, so his friends made sure I heard from him.

I obeyed my mother like a good daughter. I made a point of not mentioning Seamus again to her, and she seemed to believe that I was finally over my "silly romance" with the Irish boy who stole my heart.

One day, my parents were out of town for the day. My father had business, and my mother spent her time shopping with the wives of my father's business associates. This was the perfect opportunity. Seamus took me away to our special place at the gardens, where we made plans for our future.

"Don't cry, lass. Nothing is as bad as it seems."

"You do not understand. My mother does not want me to see you again. She refuses to believe how much I love you and you love me. She's been cruel, Seamus, and with leaving for the U.S. soon, maybe it is best that we say goodbye now."

"No! Did you not believe me when I told you I loved you?"

"Of course I did. You know I do."

"That is what I thought. I have never felt this way about anyone before you crashed into my life. Our age does not matter, only what we feel in our hearts. I would never hurt you, and no matter how much your mother tries to convince you of that, she is wrong. I would die for you, Shaena. You must believe me. I will be going off to study at the university in the fall. When I complete my studies, you will be of age and could do or be with anyone you want. I am hoping you choose me to be that person. I will wait for you. You have my promise, my love. Your family may be able to control you now, but they will not have that power forever. Come back to me the minute you are free. I will wait for you. I love you. Come back to Kildare. I will be here waiting with my arms open for you, my beautiful Shaena. Trust me. Believe in what we have. Believe in love, and I promise you, I will give you the fairy tale you have been dreaming about."

"I love you, Seamus O'Toole. I will come back to you. I promise."

He crushed his lips down to mine and kissed me after all the promises he had just said to me. I never wanted to let him go.

And that's when I heard the sound of my father behind us. Our connection was broken with my mother physically separating us.

"You abominable child! I knew I could not trust you! The first opportunity you get, and you run to him. You are a liar, and I will make sure you understand what it feels to betray me like this," mother hissed at me as she looked at Seamus with disgust.

"Mrs. Blake, you have it all wrong. We have done nothing wrong. I love your daughter, and she loves me. What crime have we committed? Please don't do this to her," Seamus begged my mother for mercy, but it was no use.

My father pulled me by my arm and placed me in the back of the waiting car. He told my mother to join me, and after shooting cold daggers at Seamus, she did. I was crying and calling out to him from the window, but my mother held me back. Our hands touched for only a brief moment before we were separated once again.

I heard my father tell Seamus that this would be the last time he would ever see me. Seamus tried to reach for my hand, but my father put his hands up to stop him. My love never gave up even when my parents tried to stop him. Seamus pleaded with my father to listen to him, but it was no use when he had made his decision. We would be leaving first thing in the morning.

As our car pulled away, I called out to him from the window, "I'm sorry. I love you, Seamus. I'm so sorry."

He called out for me as loud as his voice allowed him to and professed his love for me. Our driver hit the brakes at my father's request, and he jumped out to stop Seamus from running after us. My father grabbed Seamus by his shirt and shoved him off. He told him to stop his madness and just let us drive away before anyone gets hurt. Seamus showed no fear and challenged my father.

He said, "I love her, Mr. Blake. Why are you doing this? She is your daughter! What kind of father treats his own flesh and blood like this? You should be ashamed of yourself! Between your hostility and her mother's hatred for me, God knows what I did to deserve this to cause Shaena so much pain. Tell me why! Because we love each other?"

My father looked remorseful but told Seamus to go home and forget about me. I hit and shoved at my father when he returned to the car, but he held me in place and allowed me to cry. I watched helplessly as Seamus ran after our car again, but soon we were out of sight, and my heart was shattered into thousands of pieces.

Damn you, mother! Damn you. I know why I had to listen to you, but even with your threats, I did not have to believe you for as long as I did.

I cried and cried reliving my past with Seamus, soaking my pillow with my tears. I said a silent prayer for wherever he was in the world today and that he was happy, and the cruelty he endured at the hands of my parents had been forgotten, along with memories of me. I never wanted to cause him any pain, but my love for him did, my mother made sure of it.

A knock at the door startled me. The door opened, and it was Aideen.

"Oh, Ms. Blake, are you alright? I was just passing by and heard you crying. What can I do for you?"

"Forgive me, Aideen, I am embarrassed. With how old these castle walls are, I never imagined anyone hearing me."

"You would be surprised. Now, if you please, would you tell me what is troubling you to the point of crying? I can call for some tea. Would you like some? It may help."

"I wish it could, but no, thank you."

"You didn't touch your dinner."

"I wasn't hungry. I cannot seem to concentrate and steady my thoughts in this place. My mind has not been able to calm since I stepped off the plane."

"You mean here at Barberstown?"

"No, not here, it's Kildare. When I was fifteen, I lived here with my parents, and it was probably the happiest time in my life."

"Ireland has a way of doing that. It is a magical place. How long did you live here?"

"A year. I never wanted to leave, but I was forced to, and because of my young age, I had no choice but to go with my parents."

"That sounds awful, I'm sorry."

"I am too, more than you know. You are easy to talk to. I never had a comfortable rapport where I could share like this with my mother. She never had time to bother. Oh god! I must sound so silly to you. Here I am, the day before the meeting that will make my professional career, and I am crying over my depressing relationship with my mother. I am sorry."

"Please don't apologize. I have three children of my own who are all grown now and out in the world being independent. I divorced their father after my third child was born. I was hopeful our marriage could survive, but it did not work out the way I imagined. I raised my daughters and son on my own, right here at Barberstown. I was a friend of the current owner, and he took us in when I had no place to go. Looking back now, it was the best decision I ever made in my life. Getting out of a loveless marriage and finding myself again was refreshing. How could I ever expect my children to respect me when I had no faith in myself, remaining in a relationship with a man who just didn't want me anymore or the children he made with me?"

"I'm so sorry, Aideen."

"Don't be, Shaena. It all worked out in the end, and I have never been happier. My children are well-adjusted, and I couldn't be more proud of each of them. This is their time to discover what makes them happy, and I am doing what makes me happy."

"And that would be tending to emotional American women who cry too loudly?"

"Exactly. That is number seven in my contract."

"Thank you for talking with me. I guess I needed to vent a bit. I assure you, I will not cry tomorrow."

"No worries, my new friend," she said, giving me a big hug. "I will have tissues sent to your room immediately, just in case."

"You said Weston James wasn't scary, so I may hold off on the tissues. You could always send wine instead!"

"I will make a note of that dear. Get some sleep and dream of good things," she said, offering me another hug.

"I will, Aideen. I know exactly what I will dream about tonight."

"Someone special, I hope."

"Yes, very special," I said as I closed my door.

Once upon a time, I was happy and loved by a boy with curly red hair and a dusting of freckles. I prayed for a long time that, even in the briefest of moments, he knew I had felt the same for him.

I still had the purple rose he gave to me on the day he told me he loved me. It was pressed between the pages of one of my favorite books. My mother did not get to take everything away from me that day. Whenever I felt most alone, which was quite often, I would run my fingers over the flower, and take comfort in knowing I still had a small part of him with me.

FOUR

Old Ghosts

I read somewhere that once your brain sleeps, dreams are a way of reliving your life when you have no control over stopping what re-plays in your mind. I only believed that theory to be true when nights like last night happened.

Dreaming of my past confused me even more. The memories of my time with Seamus were all around me. Anywhere I turned, he was there. Our relationship was in secret for nearly the year I had known him. We felt it would be better not having to explain ourselves to the doubters who did not believe in us. My mother was one of them. She had been snooping in my room one day, and then confronted me with a barrage of questions. I had no choice but to be honest with her. The only thing was, she did not want to hear the ramblings of a silly schoolgirl who led with her heart instead of her mind.

She was right to some extent. I did lead with my heart and was not ashamed of it. I may have wanted more with Seamus, but it never went beyond the boundaries of young love. He treated me with the utmost respect. He knew I was younger, and never would do anything to hurt me. But my mother was convinced he was some predator that would just use me and leave me for scraps. I was so brainwashed back then into believing, that everything she said was truth. Thinking about it all again hurt my heart.

I believed when my father died, he also left this world with a broken heart. They never kissed, touched, or even danced with each other. They were too prim and proper for public displays of affection. Even my father's funeral felt staged and rehearsed. He suffered a heart attack at his office one afternoon, and to think about it now, I do not recall ever witnessing my mother cry over his loss. He was her husband, and yet she never showed an ounce of emotion or remorse for how she treated him when he was alive.

I was in my first year at Brown when I received the call about my father. I could not speak. I cried for the next five days. Mother was her usual self. She put on the brave face and played the mourning widow, and less than two weeks later, we were sitting in their lawyer's office to hear the reading of the will. My mother was left the majority of his estate, with my portion in a trust until I turned twenty-five, and then I would be free to live any way I cared to. My father made sure his family would remain in the lifestyle he always provided, but all I wanted was my father to be alive. I could care less about the money, but mother once again laughed at me.

"Love does not pay the bills, my dear daughter. Love does not keep you from freezing in the cold winter months." These lovely words of wisdom I endured for the next hour, until I left for school.

The next few years were lonely for me, but I managed to graduate with honors and earn my degree. My passion was for the written word. I loved English Literature, and Jane Austen was my favorite. I would read until my eyes would burn from exhaustion, but I loved it. It was no wonder why I had chosen to go in to publishing. I thrived off the adrenaline that would course through my body when immersed in a manuscript and my heart raced with excitement. My expertise was working with indie writers who were considered "the little engines that could" on *The New York Times'* bestsellers list.

I wondered if Aideen could send up a masseur before my meeting with Weston James, but there wasn't enough time. My muscles were stiff from the way I slept. I tossed and turned until I finally was comfortable, and now it was morning. I got up from the four-poster canopy king-sized bed, and did a stretch. I was afraid to look at my reflection.

I looked in the mirror before my shower. My reflection was exactly what I was expecting after a night of bawling my eyes out. Was I in a boxing match with Rocky? My eyes would confirm it. Anytime I cried, my face would get red and my eyes would form dark purple circles underneath them. Where was Jesse when I needed him? He could probably fix my face with makeup if he were here, but I was on my own so no luck there.

Aideen said that Weston was not scary, which made me laugh now because I was the one who looked scary. *Hi, Mr. James, my name is Shae, and I like to turn into a zombie when pitching to new clients.* Yeah, I have to work on my appearance before leaving this room.

I stayed underneath the showerhead until the water turned cold. It was quite refreshing after my first night back in Kildare.

I took some calming breaths, which always seemed to help, and then I worked on my hair. It took me nearly an hour to dry it. It was on the thicker side but pin straight down my back. I pulled my hair back into a French braid, and then tucked the tail of it underneath into a sophisticated style. I had chosen my navy blue suit, accompanied with a string of pearls. I was not one for heavy makeup. I always wore mascara, and I would rather pinch my cheeks for color instead of using blush. I applied a simple lip-gloss, and I was done. I stood in front of the floor-length mirror and sighed miserably. I looked like a schoolteacher on her first day of work. It was too conservative and screamed cat lady in a twenty-something-old body.

I had only thirty minutes to spare before meeting Weston. I needed help and fast. I opened up my laptop and called Jesse using Skype. It would be after one in New York, and I hoped I would catch him alone without an audience to see my disastrous ensemble.

"Hey, you! How is Ireland?" Before I could answer, he shrilled, "What are you wearing? And how did that suit end up in your luggage without my knowledge?"

"Good afternoon to you, too. I added it after you left. Is it that bad?"

"Um…yes it is. If it makes it back here to New York, I will burn it."

"Jesse, I need help. I'm supposed to meet Weston for breakfast in less than thirty minutes, and I just feel sick."

"Are you? If I had to guess, it's probably from that hideous outfit you are wearing. Please don't pan down the camera. I definitely don't want to see what shoes you paired with that."

"I need help, Jesse! No more jokes."

"Okay, I'm sorry for teasing you. Honestly, you don't look good. Ugh, it looks like you have the flu but still have to show up at your job in the law library to go shush some kids."

"Exactly. I just want to crawl under a rock and stay there. This was a mistake coming here."

"Good luck with that, because James will find you. Okay, no more time for small talk. We will catch up later, but for now, let me help you get ready. I really hope all the fabulous clothes I packed for you are hanging neatly in a closet. My heart will not recover if I see anything crumpled in your suitcase."

"Will you stop? Everything is in the closet."

"Good, now go in there and wear the wide leg wool suiting trousers, and pair them up with the sleeveless black silk camisole top. Go simple on the shoes. Wear the Louis Vuitton Eyeline pump in the nude color."

I followed Jesse's suggestions, and I heard his catcall whistle of approval once I stepped in front of my computer screen.

"Oh, honey, you look perfect! The hair still works. Lose the granny pearls, and wear the diamond stud earrings."

"What about a jacket? This place is cold."

"Skip the jacket. This freak has no chance once he sees you dressed to kill, and the cold will work in your favor. Once those nipples protrude out, I bet you could sing a tune and he wouldn't notice anything else."

"Gee, thank you for setting the women's movement back thirty years."

"Come on, Shae, that was funny, and don't bitch at me for making you beautiful."

"I miss you, Jesse. You should have come with me."

"I still can, you know."

"Let me see how my first impression goes, and then I will call you. Hey, your background looks different. Where are you?"

"Roger's condo."

"Oh, Jesse, why?"

"Why not? I called out sick today. It was no use going in and putting myself through a long day without you to help me commiserate with."

"If you would just talk with James, you would not have to hide at Roger's place. You could be with the one you truly want and be happy."

"I love you, Shae. Thanks for the call. Good luck with the freak, and word of advice to you: if you ever get a life outside of Prestige, *then* you can lecture me on relationships."

The connection was lost, and once again, I had hurt his feelings. Jesse was right. I did not know the first thing about relationships, because that part of my heart died when I left Seamus and followed my mother's lead.

I checked and double-checked my notes, and then I was ready for my meeting. Before leaving, I texted Jesse with a one-word apology: "Sorry."

I did not expect a reply in return, but he could never stay angry with me for long: "Forgiven."

With one final glance in the mirror, I left to meet Weston. Aideen greeted me at the bottom of the landing.

"Good morning, Shae. I trust you slept well."

"I did, thank you."

"You don't lie very well."

"I beg your pardon?"

"Shae, you look tired."

I blurted, "So, in other words, I look like shit?"

God! What has gotten into me? Open mouth, insert total foot for bitching at someone who has been nothing but kind to me.

"I'm sorry, Shae. I did not mean to imply anything by my observation. You look beautiful. I was just expressing concern for you. I have tissues on hand if you need them."

Oh, I really like this woman.

"I get cranky and defensive when I work on no sleep. I did not mean to snap at you, Aideen. Please accept my apology."

"No worries. How about we have a spot of tea? It always helps."

"No, thank you. I would rather wait for Mr. James to arrive."

"Fair enough. He would like you to wait in the observatory. He should be along shortly. If you should change your mind about the tea, there is a service set up in the room for you."

"Thank you so much, Aideen. You are so kind."

She escorted me to the observatory. I could not ignore the eerie feeling I felt when I entered the room. The walls felt like they had eyes. Although I have never been here before, I felt a familiar feeling drawing me in. Goosebumps covered my skin, and it had nothing to do with the temperature here at the castle. As I placed my briefcase down, I looked around the room. The structure was fitted with glass walls and a dome ceiling that looked out to the sky. The early morning sun was shining through, making the room appear to glow in an array of colors.

I began to feel more at ease and took a seat by the window overlooking the gardens and the colossal-sized greenhouse on the property.

I'm sure it housed the most beautiful flowers that would blossom here in the seasons. Ireland was a beautiful country with miles of luscious greenery.

I placed my right hand over my heart, and it felt like drums beating. Seamus used to tell me that whenever I was near, his heart would begin to race as mine was right now. It was the anticipation of meeting Weston James.

I had to imagine his agent and publishing house signed non-disclosure agreements to protect his identity. I could understand to a degree choosing to be a mystery to your readers, but at some point, wouldn't it get old? Readers want to know the person who makes them dream of bigger things, to question everything they believed to be true before they read the author's novel. They love the story behind the story, the real-life inspiration to these fantasies. They want the happily ever after, the hero who wins the girl in the end. Any other ending would destroy their hopes and dreams and probably knock their hero down a few pegs until the next novel that brings him back to worship status. And the writer is the one who creates all that. I don't understand why an author would dodge the applause and recognition, the fame and celebrity, the autographs and photo ops.

I was not sure what was keeping him. Maybe this was a test. If I waited long enough, would the pressure get to me? On the other hand, would I use my wit to control my emotions? I activated the voice memo app on my phone and began recording some notes.

"Who exactly is Weston James? Why the incessant need for privacy—a sordid past filled with scandal, perhaps? Are you just a lonely human being that prefers to remain hidden? To be exposed is scary. Are you taking a risk opening Pandora's box? Was that your intention all along?"

A voice called out from behind me.

"Interesting theory, Ms. Blake. Let's begin there, shall we?"

It was him. Weston James.

FIVE

Her Road Back to Me

Two days earlier…

"Is this a joke? Am I really speaking with Weston James?" James Gentry of Prestige Publishing questioned, only furthering my annoyance. I was regretting not having Connor make this call.

"I can assure you, it is. I have kept a close eye on your publishing house. You have successfully held your own against the top five you compete with. To be blunt, Mr. Gentry, I admire your tenacity. I would like to request your best agent to pitch to me in person on why you are the best house to represent me. Do you think you have what I am looking for?"

Mr. Gentry stumbled over his words until he finally believed this was not a dream and this call was very real. I heard the shuffling of papers, clicking keyboard sounds, and if my ears deceived me, I thought I heard a cup falling to the floor. With the chaos I had to endure speaking with him, I also found it refreshing that I could elicit such a reaction from a man whose reputation was known as a raging bull wearing a designer suit. He played a good game and strove to take on his rivals with no hesitation or lack of confidence. He was a salesman with one goal in mind: to sell, acquire, and succeed. His company had taken leaps and bounds over the last couple of years with Shaena Blake on their payroll. Yes, I knew this was right.

"Mr. Gentry, are you still there?"

"My apologies, Mr. James. I am still waiting for my brain to catch up where I can communicate clearly with you. I wasn't aware you had cut ties with Pan Macmillan."

"Contrary to the rumors, and what makes it into the American papers, my contract had reached its end with my UK publishing house, and I was free to pursue other outlets best suited for my needs. Mr. Gentry, I assure you, I have my pick of any number of publishing houses in the world to represent me and my work, but I am seeking a specific individual for a specific project in mind."

"Fair enough, Mr. James. I will give some thought on who would be best, and I will get back to you."

"Not necessary, I already know who I want."

"You do? Okay, who is it?"

"Shaena Blake," I said with a smile across my face. "Is she not your best?"

"She is, Mr. James. I am just so taken with your knowledge of my company and who I employ."

"I make it my business to know everything about anyone I work with. My circle of trust is very small, and I expect complete discretion when working with me. You do understand that, don't you?"

"Of course, sir."

"Wonderful, so if there is nothing else, I will have my assistant e-mail you my instructions detailing all that I want. I expect this conducted in an expedited manner. I will see Ms. Blake the day after tomorrow."

"Excuse me, Mr. James, but where am I sending Ms. Blake to?"

"Kildare."

"Kildare? As in..."

"Ireland. Is there any other? I expect to see Ms. Blake in Kildare in two days. All will be explained in the packet that will be sent over shortly to you via-email. Do not fail me. I am not one who tends to make requests such as this one, and I am not one for hearing the word, no."

I ended my call with James Gentry, and kicked my feet up on my desk. I could not escape the feeling of satisfaction that was strumming through me as I ended my call.

It was not too often that an editor-in-chief was given the gift I placed in his hands. I would allow him to revel in championing me. I was quite sure he was dancing around his office just about now, as he believed this was a victory in securing me as a client, but he could not be more wrong.

A few moments later, Connor entered my study.

"Have you sent the packet to Mr. Gentry at Prestige?" I asked.

"I have, sir."

"And the arrangements at Barberstown?"

"All in place, sir. Ms. McGann is quite good at her job. I trust Ms. Blake's needs will all be met."

"Leave her needs to me."

"One last time, sir, are you sure about this?"

"I am, Connor. I have never been surer in all of my life. I will not waste one more day hidden in my tower."

"Sir, all preparations for your guest are in place. Will there be anything else you require before I take my leave?"

"You've done well, Connor. Thank you for all of your assistance. You will collect Ms. Blake in Dublin, bring her to me, and I will take it from there. That will be all."

He hesitated with his departure before turning back.

"Is there something else?" I questioned him.

"Sir, forgive me in choosing to be forward, especially at this time, but I was just wondering if you were having any reservations about Ms. Blake. Once you reveal your identity to these Americans, there will be no going back. You have always maintained complete anonymity when it comes to your work and personal life, and now..."

"Go on, Connor. And now…what?"

"Forgive me, sir, I have overstepped."

"I'm intrigued. Finish your sentence. I insist." Today was not the day to fuck with my mind.

"I was merely stating that you have flourished under the radar. Your recent actions have raised alarms with staff and the precious few who work day and night to protect what you are now exposing. How will you know if you can trust an outsider like Ms. Blake, an American literary shark who probably cares more about a signed contract than the author himself?"

"I appreciate your concerns, and they have been respectfully noted, but you needn't worry about me, Ms. Blake, and her intentions. I am well aware of who I have invited into my life, but for now, you will have to trust me."

"I do, sir, but that doesn't mean I will not worry. These years have not been easy for you, and I have been there for every setback you have had to endure. You are finally in a position where all has been returned to its rightful place. I would not want anything or anyone to interfere with that."

"Connor, your concerns are noted and are not necessary when they come to Ms. Blake. My reasons for remaining behind the veil were necessary back then, but now it is time to step out from the protected boundaries of these walls and live again."

My explanation seemed to satisfy Connor, my faithful assistant from the beginning of my writing career. He had seen me at my worse, from my darkest days when I feared there would be no light in my life, to the moments of accolades that were bestowed upon me.

Connor was unsure of Ms. Blake's intentions, but it was I who initiated this introduction, so why be untrusting? The writing world could be a lonely place. For some, all you had were your thoughts, which became the words that many seemed to believe defined you. But the ones I wrote had actually been a message in a bottle that I hoped would be found by only one person.

My heart practically bled out when writing *The Vanishing Raven*. Those words were really meant for the one who was in my heart and wrapped into the deepest depths of my soul. I never expected that my single intention would reach and affect thousands around the world. As a result, I became more withdrawn and maintained anonymity. But the loneliness was becoming unbearable.

I walked over to the mirror and took in my appearance. The man staring back at me was not one she would know. She would see what no one had before. She would see me as if for the first time. I was hoping she could look beyond the face and a connection would be felt.

All would be revealed in time with Ms. Blake of Prestige Publishing. She would be the only one I would allow to see the real me.

The Vanishing Raven was about to return home.

Yesterday...

As much as I willed myself to stay away until the morning, I could not help to steal a glance or two at the beautiful Shaena Blake. She was everything I imagined her to be. She was taller than her natural height, wearing four-inch killer stilettos. Dressed professionally in a business suit, I could only fantasize what was underneath.

Her hair was dark as night, flowing straight down to the middle of her back, and perfectly trimmed with the utmost precision. I observed from the shadows her introduction with Ms. McGann and the obvious coldness she endured from Connor. She appeared to handle him, but I was angered with him for not following my orders. How dare he treat a guest whom I have invited to my home in that manner? We would most certainly be having a discussion soon on his behavior.

She blossomed under Aideen's kindness, almost blushing with crimson. I left her in very capable hands and set out to find Connor, who was effectively evading my questions when I finally found him. He was going through some papers, seated behind my desk, as I made my way into the study, slamming the door behind me.

"How dare you, Connor! How dare you?"

I was enraged over his treatment of Ms. Blake, to the point of grabbing him by his lapels and hauling him from my chair. He stumbled a bit, but maintained his balance.

"Sir, if you would allow me to explain before thrashing me again, I would so appreciate it."

"I will not allow anything. Were my instructions not clear to you? How dare you speak to her in that way? And continue to be incredibly cold and dismissive?"

"Sir, I mean no disrespect to you or to Ms. Blake, but this is a colossal mistake on your part. You know nothing of her. She is ruthless. I have met women like her before, especially in this business. She will not stop at anything to gain your trust for the sake of your name on her client list. We have been over this a thousand times. I have stated all of my misgivings, but you still choose to ignore them. Why? You have never doubted my judgment before, and now all that I say is wrong and not welcomed by you."

I let out the deep breath I was holding and sat down behind my desk. My hands were shaking to the point that I needed to squeeze them into tight fists.

"Connor, you have been my most trusted friend over these last few years, but your concerns over Ms. Blake are simply unjustified. You cannot possibly imagine what I have been through the last six years of my life. I have lived in my own private hell, surrounded by a fortress that no one can get through. I have suffered unimaginable pain having to go through twenty-seven surgeries. Between the rehabilitation and yearning to feel human again, I am finally at a comfortable place, and here you stand in my way of rejoining the land of the living? Why are you so determined to stop me?"

"It is not my intention, and I do not need a reminder of what you have been through. I was there, remember?"

"You were, and for all of it. This is why you, of all people, should understand why this is so important to me."

"I do, sir, more than you know. But you've been hurt before, and now bringing Ms. Blake here may not be in your best interest."

"I will decide what is best for me. All I am asking of you is to trust me, and believe I know exactly what I am doing especially when it comes to her. You are my friend—probably my best and only—but if you cannot do what I expect of you, then I believe our friendship has found its ending and we must part ways—not only in friendship, but in business as well."

"You don't mean that."

"Have you ever known me to not say what I feel? Get on board, Connor, or get out. It is your choice."

He let out a sigh, and walked over to the bar to fix himself a drink.

"Fine, I'm in. I will not do anything else to distress Ms. Blake. I apologize."

Although he said all the right words, I could not help the look of betrayal on his face. I was my own man and had my own back. I knew where my heart was leading me to, and no one would ever stand in my way again.

"I accept your apology, and Connor, thank you."

He said nothing more, and left me alone to my thoughts about her: Shaena Blake, who now simply went by "Shae."

I wondered why she shortened her name. I was sure I would discover many things about the beautiful maiden who had traveled many miles across the oceans to meet me.

As usual, I was lost in my thoughts and time got away from me. Connor had retired for the evening, and I was once again alone.

I wondered about her. Had she eaten yet? I knew my time was approaching to come face-to-face with Ms. Blake, but that still did not stop me from trying to get close to her without being discovered. I quietly walked to where her suite was, and I listened against the door. I heard crying coming from the other side. I was alarmed and worried for her. I could not just knock on her door or break it down, as that was where my mind was leading me. I had to think quickly. I knew my patience would wear thin before her tears would stop. Why was she crying? I had to know.

I called Ms. McGann immediately and asked her to check on Ms. Blake. She said she would do so at once. I waited for a few minutes. When I saw her quickly walking down the hallway to her room, I stepped back into the shadows but remained close enough so I could listen.

After a few attempts to get Ms. Blake's attention, she finally opened the door with swollen eyes and flushed cheeks. Dammit! She *was* crying, and from what I could observe by her appearance, she looked very sad.

"Oh, Ms. Blake, are you alright? I was just passing by and heard you crying. What can I do for you?"

Oh, she was good. Aideen was quick on her feet and sounded convincing.

"Forgive me, Aideen. I am embarrassed. With how old these castle walls are, I never imagined anyone hearing me."

"You would be surprised. Now if you please, would you tell me what is troubling you to the point of crying?"

They were still in the doorway, where I could hear all that was said between them. A few moments later, Shaena stepped aside, gestured with her hand, and granted entrance for Aideen to enter.

As I continued to listen, her tears stopped and were replaced with laughter. Sending Aideen in was the right thing to do. I remained where I was for the next hour or so, trying to listen to as much as I could of their conversation. When I heard movement closer to the door, I once again stepped into the shadows. I witnessed a happier Shaena. She hugged Aideen, and both women smiled. I could hear her clearly now, as I was so close in her proximity. She was smiling brightly, which pleased me to no end.

I watched Aideen give her one more hug, and then Shaena closed her door. I let out the breath I had been holding, and for the first time in a long time, I knew I would also find some peace in my dreams tonight. I smiled at the thought of it.

"My sweet Shaena, I am far from being scary. You will see the real me soon enough. Sleep soundly and dream of purple roses and walks through the gardens. I promise that after tomorrow, you shall not shed another sad tear again. Until then, Shaena."

Today...

I imagined my entrance differently than how I just entered the observatory, but I could not contain my excitement when I heard her voice. She was nervous, a bit unsure of herself, not the "literary shark" I expected her to be. This was how Connor described and judged her as. He was wrong in his assessment. She was beautiful, intelligent, and her innocence gave her away. Designer clothes and fancy hair-dos could only hide so much. She was suffocating in those confines.

My sudden arrival startled her. She nearly dropped her phone to the ground but was too quick and caught it. As if she was looking in a mirror, she nervously checked her appearance before turning around to face me. It was a refreshing sight to observe.

"I apologize, Mr. James. I was taking some notes for our meeting."

"No apologies necessary, Ms. Blake. Welcome to my home. I am Weston James, and I am delighted you could make the trip on such short notice."

"Home? You live here? As in this is your castle?"

Oh my goodness! She was delightful. It was not necessary for her to be nervous.

"As a matter of fact, I occasionally do live here, Ms. Blake. I am not the sole owner of Barberstown Castle, more like a silent partner. I stay here when I need to be surrounded by beauty."

"Beauty is an understatement," I heard her say under her breath, making me delighted once more.

The lovely Ms. Blake was very enchanting and added beauty of her own to this centuries old castle!

"Shall we sit? Tea perhaps?" I asked.

"I would love a cup."

I poured her cup and handed her the tea. She politely accepted and said thank you.

"My pleasure, lassie." As the term of endearment slipped from my lips to her ears, I watched her expression turn to surprise, and possibly reminding her of a memory long forgotten.

A moment later, the teacup with scolding hot water crashed to the floor, with the water splashing on her pant leg. I was terrified that she may be hurt.

"Ms. McGann..." I called out for assistance.

Ms. McGann rushed in, followed by Connor.

"Mr. James, are you alright?" Connor asked and completely ignored the fact that Ms. Blake was holding the bottom of her leg. She looked in pain, probably burned from the water.

"Yes, I am fine. Do you not see that Ms. Blake is hurt? Call for a doctor at once."

"Yes, sir."

"Mr. James, I am sure it's nothing. My fault for acting so clumsy."

"You always were. It was one of the qualities that I loved about you," I slipped out.

My thoughts were off and running before I could stop them. She looked questionably at me but remained quiet.

"Please, may I have a look?"

"Of course, but I am sure you are all overreacting."

I gently lifted her pant leg to see her alabaster skin turn to a shiny pink where the water splashed her. Her trousers were not at full length, and just her luck the water hit her skin where the cuff cut off.

"I am far from overreacting, Ms. Blake. You have a second-degree burn beginning to rear its ugly head. The doctor should be here at any moment to treat this for you. I am so sorry our first meeting has begun this way."

"Mr. James, it is my fault. I confess you took me by surprise when you called me 'lassie.' I had not heard that reference in a long time, and it just reminded me of someone. Please do not apologize again. How about you just call me Shae?"

"Fair enough. I will call you Shae if you call me Weston."

"You have a deal."

She shook my hand, and it took all my self-control not to lean down and place a kiss on her soft skin. I could feel my touch elicit a physical reaction. My thumb grazed over hers, as we remained connected. She began to warm, her cheeks changed color before my eyes, and all by one touch. I knew I needed to pull back my hand before I had completely given myself away, but this was why I had sent for her.

As I stared at her lovely features, I could not help but get lost in her eyes. Those gorgeous green eyes of hers told a story, one I wished to learn more about.

Finally, we both came to our senses with the interruption of Dr. Collins stepping into the room, carrying his medical bag with him. Ms. McGann made the introductions, and I stepped aside for him to treat Ms. Blake's leg.

I was beside myself and angry with Connor for his lack of concern. He had remained back and out of my sight while Dr. Collins treated Ms. Blake.

"There now, all better. You were lucky, dear. Your clothing absorbed most of the water. You just have a small patch of skin affected with a second-degree burn. I will leave this antibiotic cream with you. Keep the area clean, and apply with a clean dressing for the next few days. In a few weeks, it will just be a memory."

"Thank you, Dr. Collins, for all of your help."

"My pleasure dear. You take care now."

He seemed comfortable with his exam, but I was far from okay. Just the thought of any inch of her delicate skin left damaged just wrecked me.

"Dr. Collins, are you sure she will not be left with a scar?"

My obvious concern was not easy to hide. All eyes were on me as I voiced my question. The good doctor kept his answer simple, assured me that Ms. Blake would be fine and left with no scars. I let out a sigh of relief. I was hanging on by a thread and knew I needed to get some air before my anxiety got the best of me.

I had Ms. McGann escort the doctor out of the observatory, and my look to Connor spoke volumes on how displeased I was with him. Ms. Blake patted her leg and kept her head hanging down low. She didn't do a great job at hiding her feelings, and clearly, she looked em-barrassed. I wanted to give her comfort but held back until we could begin this meeting again. When she finally looked up, she had glazed over eyes, which nearly shattered me.

"Weston, I apologize for my less than graceful impression. I only will ask you not to judge my publishing house based on how we met. I am usually more refined than what you saw earlier."

She then stood tall with her shoulders back, appearing to be more confident after she apologized. Another pang to my heart.

"Ms. Blake—excuse me—Shae, I have already judged your house, and I have not begun to account for you yet."

She looked surprised by my statement, which left me back-peddling a bit. That was forward on my part, and not exactly what I was trying to convey to her. The spilling of tea and china breaking was not an issue; I only cared that she was hurt. She appeared determined to move forward and get down to business. I approached her and stood in her space, effectively seeing a shift in her breathing. I would have loved to know what she was thinking.

"Let us forget the tea mishap, and allow me to walk you to your room. Your leg must be stinging, and you should rest up."

"I would rather not, if it's all the same to you. My leg is fine. Can we just begin again?" she said. Her tone had changed as well as her stance.

Okay, Ms. Blake, game on.

"Of course we can. Are you hungry?" I asked.

"Starved."

After Aideen reported to me last night that she had missed dinner, I was concerned. She already looked thin to me. I was prepared to put up a fight and was thankful she was willing to eat.

"Me too," I replied. "Shall we have lunch since we have missed our suitable breakfast time? I will have Ms. McGann come back in, and please order anything your heart desires. I shall return in a few minutes."

"Sounds great. Thank you."

"The pleasure is all mine, Shae."

While we were both calmer, I took the opportunity to take her hand once again, but this time I brought it up to my mouth where I could kiss it. She shyly smiled but did not pull away, blossoming once again under my touch.

"Thank you, Ms. Blake, I've been waiting to do that."

She remained quiet, and I left her to her thoughts, which I could only imagine should be running rampant now.

As my heart raced with excitement after leaving Shae on her own for a bit, I would not ignore my anger with Connor. I summoned him at once to my study. He entered and closed the door behind him, taking a seat in front of my desk.

"Connor, this will be the last time we have this conversation. What is your problem? Do not sit here and evade my question. I saw the look in your eyes when they were stabbing Ms. Blake. Why? She has done nothing wrong to you, and yet you have this obvious animosity toward her. Would you feel the same if I had extended an invitation to her boss instead of her?"

"I told you last night that I would no longer upset Ms. Blake, and I have not. Just because I am not smiling like a lovesick fool as you are doing, does not mean I am behaving in a cruel manner. Frankly, I am offended."

"Lovesick fool? Is that how you see me? A man cannot be kind without being perceived as foolish? A man cannot enjoy morning tea with a woman without perceived as ridiculous?"

"Your words, not mine, Weston. The entire plan you have devised to bring Ms. Blake here has not gone according to the way you had hoped it would. Do you know she spent practically the entire night crying in her room? Her cries were heard throughout the castle. It was a painful cry, Weston."

"I'm well aware of how she spent her first night here in my home. Why do you think I sent Aideen to comfort her? After they talked, Ms. Blake was fine."

"How can you say that? It is obvious how uncomfortable she is here. We all see it; all but you. Back in the observatory, her actions spoke volumes. I can draw up a contract for a one-book deal and have Prestige represent you on a 'we will see how it goes' plan. All will be happy, and they get to have bragging rights that you, Weston James, are their new client...for the time being, anyway. You do not need to impress anyone. Your work will speak for itself and will rise to the top."

"Connor, first of all, I would never sign a one-book deal with any publishing house. That, my friend, is ridiculous. Secondly, you know I have no new projects to speak of, I never did. That was the lure to get Ms. Blake here. My intention is not to have her leave at the end of the week with a signed contract. I plan on having her stay forever and signing a different contract which has nothing to do with the book world."

"Yes, I know. I know you have waited a long time for this day, but have you taken into account that she may not give you the answer you want? Weston, you must prepare yourself for the latter outcome. If Ms.

Blake says no to your request, what then? Another broken heart that may never recover this time around. As for the book deal, what about the sequel to *The Vanishing Raven*? We discussed this Weston, and I believed you when you said it was written. This is why I suggested the one-book deal. It is smart and will appease Ms. Blake and Prestige."

He continued, "Please, Weston, as your friend—and I speak only as your friend—this is why I am not one hundred percent on board with your plan, because I truly do not think you have considered all of the alternatives. I know you believe all I care about is your success, and the privileges I get to enjoy because of you, but I was your friend first and business partner second. I have been devoted to you from day one, and you have always listened. But now I feel disengaged from all sides."

"I'm sorry you feel that way, but that is your problem, not mine. I have given everything to everyone, and now it is time for something for me. If I never write a single word again, I will be fine. You are the only one that knows the truth behind *The Vanishing Raven*. The real ending of that story has not been written yet, because I need to live it first and see how it plays out. I have lived my life in private for far too long now. My parents are gone. I have no siblings, nor family to share my life with, and being alone does not work anymore. It never did. There was a time when my work was all I needed to keep going because it served a purpose, and now it has come full-circle with Ms. Blake's arrival. We have exhausted this argument, and I do not wish to have it again with you."

He stared at me and finally responded, "Consider the matter closed. Please accept my real apology this time. You are more than capable of choosing your path, and who you want to walk beside you, maybe it's time I find one too."

Finally, he saw the light!

"Why not ask Aideen to join you for lunch? I would bet money she would be happy to go," I said to him.

"Do you really think so?"

"I do. I write romance for a living, remember? I can tell you enjoy each other's company when you are not spending so much time on my life. You will see, my friend. Maybe it is time *you* get the girl. Call it your first step to finding your path."

"Thank you, sir. Good luck, sir. I truly hope all works out for you and for Ms. Blake."

"Oh, it will, my friend. Fate has a way of bringing what is meant to be in your life, and the fragile heart will decide who stays."

After Connor took his leave, I unlocked my safe where I kept two special keepsakes. One was the first edition of my novel, *The Vanishing Raven*. The second was a picture of the Raven herself. She appeared to be daydreaming, gazing over the beautiful flowers. Glamour surrounded her, but she was the real beauty in this picture. Her hair was whooshing in the wind and her eyes cast down with a smile on her face.

And now, years later, the Raven had returned to where she had always belonged.

SIX

Pull

Shaena

After my less than graceful introduction to Weston, I returned to my room to change my clothes. I would have loved to put on a pair of comfy yoga pants, but Jesse would die knowing I did that. I felt foolish to call him again with wardrobe help, so I tackled my outfit myself.

Meeting Weston was a complete blur. After the tea fiasco, chaos erupted, and I had a doctor tending to my shin. I did not believe we even really had a conversation. I knew I was unexperienced when it came to the do's and don'ts of dating, but I wasn't blind when a guy was flirting with me. The way Weston spoke, and then his soft touches to my hand, had me in a tailspin of emotions that I didn't understand.

I removed my pants and the dressing Dr. Collins had placed on the burn. It was probably too soon to remove the bandage, but I never got a good look of my leg with how Weston reacted when the hot water splashed it. The look on his face was panic and fear. As if he suffered something similar, but more severe at the same time.

Had I not reacted so clumsily when he called me "lassie," maybe this would not have happened. In all my time spent in Ireland when I was younger, no one called me by that name other than Seamus. He would be the only one I would want to hear it from. When he said it, it meant something to me. Weston also said something else, but quickly covered it up.

What did he say again?

My leg and my head as well were beginning to throb with pain. I reapplied the bandage and took the pain pill Dr. Collins had left with me. He said it was a bit stronger than one ibuprofen.

After deciding on my outfit, I went with a wrap dress. I loved this dress. It was a lovely shade of sapphire. Jesse always teased me when I said that because he just goes with navy blue, but I prefer sapphire. I have many pieces in my wardrobe with that color, which reminded me of a certain pair of beautiful eyes I fell in love with.

Enough! No more reliving the past, at least not today.

Of course, I was not looking where I was going and crashed into the vanity table. God, I was clumsy!

Clumsy…like the day I crashed into Seamus.

He was standing on his feet with his hand extended for me to take. Once I was on my feet and feeling embarrassed from my display of clumsiness, I whispered, "Sorry."

"For what? You do not have anything to be embarrassed for. How do you know I wasn't paying any mind and crashed into you?"

Oh. My. God. I remembered what Weston said when I spilled the tea.

"Mr. James, I am sure it's nothing. My fault for acting so clumsy."

"You always were. It was one of the qualities that I loved about you."

No! My mind was playing tricks on me.

No! No! No! It was not him. It was this place playing with my mind.

He was familiar, that was all. They didn't even look anything alike. I think. I didn't get a good look at him, on account of burning my leg with the stupid tea.

My heart began to beat faster. My anxiety was building. I was now up on my feet and pacing the room, racking my brain from the moment I was in the War Room with James to when I was in the observatory with Weston. When James announced his news, I was skeptical from the beginning, but I came here anyway against what my gut was telling me.

This did not happen in my line of work. Even the grandest of divas, and believe me I had worked closely with some, did not behave the way Mr. James had. It was as if I was being courted and he was pulling at all the stops to wine and dine me. As an agent, trying to land a potential client, my job called for that, not the other way around. The room began to spin, and I felt the walls beginning to close in.

Get a hold of yourself, Shae! I always had an overactive imagination. God knows mother accused me of it every day of my existence.

This did not make sense, not at all. I had to get out of here. I needed to clear my head, take a walk to think, but where could I go? I held my head in frustration, with my anxiety taking hold of me. I left it to chance and replaced my heels with flats. My heart was leading me away from here, and I needed comfortable shoes to do so.

I managed to get to the entryway without the staff taking notice or my bodyguard, Connor. He seemed to be everywhere I was.

The air was brisk, but I welcomed it. It felt refreshing on my face as I walked on the grounds. I easily found the greenhouse, where the most gorgeous flowers in the world were. I took a seat on one of the benches and closed my eyes to think. I breathed in the array of scents from the roses as I reminisced.

"*Look what I have in my hands...a copy of* The Vanishing Raven,*" Jesse said as he made his way into my office.*

"*Let me see, let me see.*"

I was like a child in a candy shop, waiting to get my hands on the treat.

"*Don't get your panties in a twist, girl. Let me read you some excerpts first.*"

"*Jesse, you are killing me! Hand over that book.*"

"*No. Okay, so it says:*

Love was found. Love had grown. Love was pure. Our love was new...The beautiful raven appeared and collided with my heart. From the minute we touched, I knew we would never part...The raven had disappeared from my eyes but left an everlasting mark on my soul. She promised to return to me someday, I vowed to keep my promise and love no other. I would wait forever for her...

Each night my eyes will close, and I will dream of only you. You are close to my heart. I can feel you against me...Your cries broke me as they took you away, a sound I vowed never to forget. The ones that hurt you: they will suffer the same pain they bestowed on you, and all they will have is their regrets...Until we meet again, my beauty. I long for the day of your return and for my arms to hold you once more.

"*Women really go for this shit?*" *Jesse asked as he handed me the book.*

I smiled and happily began flipping through the pages. It was exquisite. I was holding a literary treasure in my hands, all the while my best friend could not appreciate what I believed this was. It was a pure tale of unrequited love: two lovers torn apart, destined to mourn over their shared loss.

"*Jesse, how can you not love this? It is beautiful beyond measure.*"

"*Yeah, well I can think of better things to measure, and I will tonight on my date with James!*"

"You are gross."

"You love me."

"That I do, but you are still gross."

"That may be true, my friend, but I doubt James will think so after I have my way with him."

"Good luck. I hope you know what you are doing. He is our boss, and do you think it's smart to date him?"

"I'm not dating him. I am going to fuck him! And for many hours, at that, so chill out."

"You say that now, but you never know when love surprises you. It can happen for you, Jesse, so do not give up on it."

"Okay, mom, I have been advised. Go read your book of unrequited love. You know, it might not hurt to find some of that of your own."

I smiled and nodded in response.

Jesse did not know that I actually had that once, and it was lost, just as the Vanishing Raven experienced. Very rarely, romance novels imitated real life. Usually, though, they were so much more fantastic and dramatic than the usual day-to-day. I guess this was why we loved them so much. We allowed ourselves to get lost for a while and forget the realities that have hurt our hearts.

I began to think about where I was…Kildare, Ireland…How beautiful the surroundings were…Barberstown Castle…How enchanted the usually reclusive Weston James was to meet me...How this whole situation was…so much more fantastic and dramatic than my usual day-to-day…

And then I remembered a conversation I had a few days ago with Jesse.

"Why me?" I asked.

"Because you are the best, and this freak knows it."

"He's not a freak. He's a genius. I know he is not your choice, but I have followed him since his first novel. His words speak to me as if he

is trying to convey a message for only me to understand. Does that sound weird to you?"

"Beyond weird, but I am sure you will love every minute of his weirdness."

This couldn't possibly be all one big production that was set up just for me. This is real life. No way.

It can't be him.

It's impossible to believe that fate would hurt me twice in my life-time.

I sat on the bench and cried out my pain. Too many memories coming back and all at once. I have to leave Ireland before I break even more.

My wastebasket was filled to the brim with crumpled letters of my ramblings of an apology. I had so much to say to Seamus, but he was not in reach anymore. Maybe he never was. Mother saw to destroying all hopes of ever making contact with him again. She watched me closely after we returned home, and if it wasn't her doing the spying, then she had Charles as her back-up.

He hated it, I knew it, but he followed orders just like my father. Anytime she would catch me with my journal, I would just say I was doing homework. Who knew if she believed me until that night when I didn't hear her come in to my room. I was wearing my headphones, and my tears had not stopped falling, reliving the look on Seamus's face when our car pulled away with him calling out for me. His cries were piercing shards of glass ripping through my heart.

"What the hell is this?" mother said.

I was startled. Her hand grabbed my wrist until I dropped the pen I was using to write my letter to him. She released me and began read-ing my letter. Even after all my suffering, she still showed no mercy. This act was a deep violation of my privacy. Why did she have to be so cruel?

"My Dearest Seamus," she relished in mocking my words. "I love you. I miss you. Please forgive me for leaving you."

Mocking turned to laughter as she stopped reading and ripped my letter in half. Then she continued to rip it into more pieces until they were so small that she threw them up into the air like confetti to further obliterate my soul.

"Why, Shaena, why? You just love to defy and deceive me. Well, you will never win, because I will always be a step ahead of you."

She grabbed my chin and held me in place so I could look up at her.

"The letter writing stops now. Do you hear me? Concentrate on your future, because this boy and the silly romance you believed you had are no more. If you are so foolish to dare to lie to me again, the consequences will be severe. And do not even attempt to run to your father about this. I will send you away so quickly, you will not have time to pack a bag. Am I clear? This is the last time I will warn you."

"Yes, mother, we are clear."

She released me and her cold eyes sent a shiver up and down my spine. My mother slammed her way out of my bedroom, but not before calling me "foolish girl," and I was alone again. This was the one certainty I had: loneliness.

I wiped my tears and sat a bit taller. As much as it pained me to relive the bad, I did have some good too. My mother pushed me every day to work hard and to stay focused on my education. I was never allowed to have friends, boyfriends, all the normality of teenager life. All I had was school, followed by college.

Yeah, bravo to you, Shae. Your life turned out just like Charlotte planned. I have degrees that hang on my wall in my big fancy office. I get to go home each night to a beautiful apartment that most dream about living in, and I have my career. My future's secured, but here's the downside: I. Am. Alone. Thank you, mother.

SEVEN

Make Her See Me

Weston

I knocked on Ms. Blake's door, but was greeted with silence in return. I slowly opened her door and made my way in, only to find her room empty. A slow panic began to rise in my heart, but I knew she had to be near. All of her things were scattered around the room. I could call for Connor or Aideen to find her, but then remembered I gave them the afternoon off to have lunch together.

I gathered my coat, scarf, and gloves and made my way outside to the cold Ireland air. It would be magical if it were to snow right about now. I walked the path that led to one of many gardens here on the property. As she came into view, my racing heart calmed, and I was delighted to see where her heart led her. She was sitting in the greenhouse with my prized roses all around her. The house contained an overabundance of purple ones, ones that always reminded me of a time long ago.

"There you are. I had wondered where you were off to," I said.

She turned to me with tears in her eyes, which painfully reminded of a time I had wished my eyes would forget, but they never did. I sat beside her, while Ms. Blake turned away from me.

"Please, look at me," I said, as I touched her shoulder and felt her tremble beneath my touch.

"I can't, Weston. You are asking the impossible, and I'm not capable of giving you what you need."

"What do you think I need from you, Shaena? I'm intrigued to know. Do I frighten you? Tell me why?"

"No, I'm not afraid. Your presence is captivating, and it makes me feel things. You make me remember a time I never thought I would ever revisit again. I am so confused, because I want to look at you, but I am struggling to believe what I am seeing."

"Look at me, Shaena. I am right here."

She wiped her eyes and did what I asked of her. Her hand removed my hat to rake her fingers through my hair. She then touched my face and felt the faint lines across my jaw line, lastly moving to my eyes.

"What do you see, Shaena?" I asked her again with my face leaning into her palm. She pulled back and stood up, turning away from me again.

"This is not happening. I will not believe it. I am not the Vanishing Raven. And you are not..."

She gripped her chest into a tight hold and had her back to me. She would not run from this, not when we were so close.

"Say it! Damn you, lassie, say it."

"I can't. I will not destroy myself again. It took too many years to put myself together again."

"You are so wrong, lass. You are still broken, and it was not you who destroyed yourself. No, a greater power had that sadistic pleasure. Please allow me to help you and free you finally. Only then will you be healed. You know, don't you? Look at me, what do you see?"

"No, I will not."

75

"You have forgotten me. Was your promise ever real? I thought it was, and I have held out hope for all of these years. And now that you have returned, you stand here denying what I always believed was real and true."

I turned her around and held her in place to look at me, to look in my eyes.

"Stop it, please. You cannot imagine how many times I read and re-read your book. It was as if you were speaking only to me. How is that possible?"

"Because I *was*! How could you not know? You had to feel the words course through your blood as they penetrated your soul. Let go, Shaena, and feel them now. Feel the intensity, the connection we have."

I gently cupped her face as more tears fell from her eyes. I wanted to kiss them away, but I could not until she broke down the walls she was hiding behind to protect her heart.

"You may not want to see who is standing in front of you, but that will not stop your heart from feeling what you know is true."

I walked over to where the purple roses were blossoming and clipped one from the planter. After carefully removing the thorns, I placed it in her hand. Her fingers tightened around the fragile stem and she closed her eyes to feel, to remember.

I said to her, "I recall a time when I was in a similar garden, but I was not alone. I was with a beautiful, young, and innocent girl. She asked me why purple roses when the gardens offered so many to choose from, but yet she was only given the purple ones."

Her eyes remained closed, but I could tell she was coming back to me. This was her way, and I gave her the time to do so.

I continued, "I could not help but smile at the girl. It was easy to do anytime I was around her. I simply asked her, don't you know? I give you the purple rose because it represents love at first sight, a love I have felt from the first moment my eyes found yours, or better yet, when your body crashed into mine."

Her tear-filled eyes were now open, and finally I saw a hint of brightness. Then sadness. She has remembered, but I still needed to hear the words.

I removed my gloves and placed my hands to her face. Her skin was soft, even tear-stained. She was still the same beautiful girl I had fallen hopelessly in love with…and still love today.

"Say it. Say the words to me. Please, Shaena, I need to hear them. Please, my love, do not make me wait one more second. Say the words."

She bit back more tears, and as I held her face, she reached for mine.

"You. You are real, and I am not dreaming, right?" she said. "You look different, but your heart is the same. Your eyes are the same. I never thought I would see you again, let alone be touching you."

Her strength was failing her, and unstoppable tears were flowing as I yearned to hear what she was struggling to say. I wiped away her tears with my thumbs as she shivered, but she did not pull away. She was close and almost there. I could feel it when we touched, and I saw it in her eyes. I gently touched her again to completely face me. Even with a tear-stained face, she was the most breathtaking beauty I have ever laid my eyes upon. She had been broken—we both were—but now it was our time for healing.

I said to her, "You don't have to be afraid. Please, say the words to make this real for both of us."

She sighed, slowly smiled, and then whispered what I longed to hear:

"The only one I have ever loved is here with me. You are Seamus O'Toole."

EIGHT

Reunion of Two Hearts, Two Souls

Shaena

"**S**eamus O' Toole," I said his name repeatedly as we remained connected with each other. "How? Why? Please explain it to me?" I questioned him between the tears that were still falling.

"I will answer all of your questions in good time, but please, allow me to hold you. I need to see you, Shaena. I need to feel your body pressed against mine. I have waited a very long time for this moment with you."

I leaned in closer, giving him permission to touch me. When I did, he pulled me as close as he could until I was completely enveloped in his arms. We remained quiet and still for a few minutes until he held my face once more.

"May I please kiss you?" he asked.

In an automatic response, I licked my lips, giving him my answer. I wanted nothing more than to feel him on me. It was as if the past years and the painful memories were gone. We were back where we left off. It felt so natural to be in his arms, to smell his scent, to feel his touch.

His face looked different. I had so many questions I wanted to ask him, but for now, I allowed myself to return to a place where I was happiest…in the arms of Seamus O'Toole.

When he had my permission, he did not hold back. His hands were tightly holding me in place as he crushed his lips down to mine in a bruising kiss. His fingers entwined through my hair and slightly pulled on my long tresses. My body felt light, as if part of my soul had just been set free again to feel what had always come naturally for us. Our breathing was heavy as we disconnected our lips, but we remained close with Seamus leaning his forehead against mine.

"I have waited so long for you. I love you, Shaena Blake. I have never stopped for all the days we were apart. I have so much to tell you, but not here. I need so much more from you than just this kiss. I need all of you. I need you in my bed. I need to claim and mark you. I need you. Please, Shaena, give yourself over to me, and we can begin again."

With Seamus still holding me, his eyes were burning through mine. My answer was yes. I could hear myself saying the words but did not feel my lips move. His eyes never left mine. He astounded me. My world turned upside-down with Weston James revealing himself to me as my true love, Seamus. My heart was pounding through my chest. He took my breath away, as I stared into his sapphire eyes. I felt dizzy with this realization about the two men, and everything all of a sudden went dark.

NINE

Trust Your Heart

Seamus

"Trust me, Shaena. I will catch you."

I carried her all the way back to the house. Aideen and Connor had returned from their lunch and witnessed me carry her up the grand staircase to my private quarters. My look to Connor should have been obvious to not even dare to interrupt me. Aideen looked concerned for Shaena, but she need not worry about my love. I would take care of her.

I placed her down onto my bed and covered her with a blanket. She looked angelic. The beautiful American girl I had fallen in love with when I was eighteen was now in my bed as a breathtakingly beautiful woman.

I climbed in beside her as gently as I could to wait for Shaena to open her eyes and see me once more. I did not want to frighten her, but I could not bear to leave her. I would never forget how we separated on the day she left Ireland and me.

"I love you, Seamus. I love you," she was screaming as loud as she could before her mother pulled her back.

When all hope was lost of catching up to her, I fell to the cold, hard ground and wept over my breaking heart. I vowed to reunite with Shaena Blake someday, and to hell with what her parents would think. They would not control her forever, and I would bide my time until we could be together again. She promised me, and I would be holding her to her word of reuniting with me, someday.

Her body stirred, and her bright sparkling eyes shot open. She sat up in the bed but was not afraid to find me next to her.

"You're here?" she questioned.

"Of course I am. Where else would I be?" I said, as I touched her face to calm her.

"Wait. Where am I? How did I get here?"

Shaena appeared to be confused until I raised myself up to my knees and held her.

"It's alright, my love. Please do not be afraid. You fainted, and I carried you back here to my room. You are safe, I promise you."

"I'm not afraid of you. I just need a minute to catch up here. Why do you look different to me, while everything else is the same as I remember?"

I kissed the top of her head and sat back on to my heels.

"I can assure you, Shaena, I am not the same physically as you knew me back then, but my heart is the same, the same one that has never stopped loving you. There was an accident, an out of this world twist of fate that was simply so cruel beyond any rhyme or reason."

"Please, tell me. I need to know everything."

"You already heard the story. I would guess you know it by heart."

"What are you talking about?"

"Don't you know? Have you not read our love story in print?"

TEN

Beyond the Reflection Staring Back at Me

Shaena

I could only imagine the expression on my face as another revelation hit my heart like a speeding truck. He reached for me, but I was already up and off the bed.

"*The Vanishing Raven*? Is that what you're referring to? I'm the Raven in your book?"

"You are," he quietly answered, confirming what I feared.

"How can I be? In the book you wrote, she left you and vowed never to return. Her love had turned cold, and she had chosen to be alone rather than live a happy life with the man she loved and made promises to. It was easier for her to break the promises than to keep them."

My eyes were on him as he got up from the bed but kept a safe distance between us.

"Didn't you, Shaena?"

"Didn't I what?"

"You broke your promise to me, Shaena. You may have had no

control when you were fifteen, but you grew up and were no longer under the watchful eyes of your parents. Therefore, as I said, you broke your promise to me. You are the Vanishing Raven because the love you had professed to me repeatedly when we were alone, somehow, you were afraid to find again when you could. You left me, and us, just to become empty shells of the lovers we once were, to exist only in our memories. That's what you did."

"We were never lovers. I was fifteen years old, and you only a few years older. I wish you had taken me then, but you never went further than kissing me, just like you did at the greenhouse."

"Shaena, just because we did not consummate what we felt for the other, does not mean we were not lovers. You were my lover the minute you allowed me to touch, kiss, and hold you. But you forgot about that, didn't you? You allowed the ones who hurt us to win."

"You are so wrong. Seamus, how could you think so lowly of me when just an hour ago you revealed how happy you were that I returned? You invited me to your bed. What kind of sick and twisted game are you playing? You write this amazing tale of lost love and aptly name it *The Vanishing Raven*, modeled by me, I come to find out. You bring me here back to Ireland under false pretenses. You reveal your identity, make me feel again—probably for the first time in over ten years—and lastly, break my heart worse than my mother ever did. I lost then, and I'm losing now, Seamus."

"It is you who are wrong, lassie. You are the one breaking me… again."

"Do not call me that. You do not get to say those words to me anymore."

"Why ever not? Does it pain your heart to hear the truth? Yes, my love, you are the Vanishing Raven who left me. You broke my heart. In your absence, I discovered a part of me that was going to love you forever, no matter what the future held. I wrote that book for you. My book was my way of communicating to you through my words, because I had no idea where you were in the world at that time. I love you, lassie. You were the one then, and the one that holds my heart to-day, and always will. You have to believe me. You have to trust me. You—we—are not lost. We found our way back to each other. Please, Shaena, look at me."

ELEVEN

Undeniable

Seamus

When her eyes met mine, there was no way of denying what her body was trying to communicate to me. Her heart wanted me. Her body wanted me. All she had to do was say the words, and I would completely hand over my soul to her.

"Say the words. Say them, Shaena."

I demanded her truth. Hell, I deserved it for what I had been through the years without her in my life! She was taken from me, and everything I had done from that time had been leading up to this moment with her now. She had to trust her heart as I asked her to do all of those years ago.

She wiped the tears from her eyes and closed the distance between us. Her body slammed up against mine, as our lips connected and tongues tangled with the other. I craved her. I wanted to taste every inch of her, and when I was through, I would begin again. As much as I longed to be inside of her, I let out my breath to regain control. I placed my hands on her hips as we kissed. She took the lead and began to remove my tie and unbutton my shirt. Her soft hands finally touched my bare skin, igniting the inner heat between us.

She pulled my shirt off. Her eyes scanned all over my upper body, as they took in every inch of me. My scars were visible. They were ugly, but the way she was looking at me, I believed she saw something other than ugliness; she saw beauty. Shaena gently kissed each scar until I nearly came and split apart in her embrace.

Next, her hands found the buckle of my belt, and once removed, she worked on my pants. Before I could even say a word, they were down at the base of my ankles. I kicked off my shoes and quickly removed my socks. Here I was, completely naked and for her to take and do as she pleased with me.

"You are beautiful, Seamus."

"It is you, my love, who is beautiful."

"How would you know that? I'm fully clothed."

"Not for long."

With her eyes teasing me with her wanton desire, the invitation was accepted, and I had my prey in sight. My deft fingers had her undressed quicker than I could say my own name. Lifting her in my arms, I placed her body in the center of my bed and began trailing my tongue beginning at her feet, where I would drop to my knees and worship at her command.

She was moving restlessly on the bed as I continued to mark every inch of her body. She was petite but molded perfectly with my frame. Her skin was silky white and flushed with every kissed placed on her. Her breasts fit perfectly in my hands, and my mouth found her erected nipples, where I feasted on them one at a time. Shaena arched her back and nearly knocked me over with her pelvis. Her arousal dripping from her sex ignited me to delve my tongue into her hot heat. Her fingers latched onto my hair, and she pulled harder with each thrust of my tongue penetrating her.

"Please, Seamus, no more. I need you inside of me."

"Patience, my love, we waited this long, you could wait one more min..."

I could not finish my sentence because of Shaena pulling me closer to her as she climaxed from one orgasm to another. My body shook from her physical reaction. I could wait no more. My hands parted her thighs, and I entered her deeply, as her legs wrapped around my waist.

Our bodies became one as we marked the other. She was mine, and I was hers, now and forever. This was what I'd hoped for. I would silently pray that she would want the same. She would want me as I was now, and not the memory from years ago.

"Shaena, look at me. Do not pull away from our connection as we come together."

Her fists clenched the sheet, and that was all I needed to lose myself inside of her.

"I love you. I love you. I love you, Shaena Blake with all of my heart. You are mine, my love, you always were, and forever shall be."

I lost myself inside of her. My body was racking with spasms as I continued to empty myself into her. Her legs tightened around me, igniting me to go again. Her eyes brightly danced with my ability to get hard again and repeat what we just did. I pulled out and then pushed in harder. I held on for as long as I could until I erupted once more, my seed spilling out from her. She was full of my come, and I never was more satisfied.

My arms gave way, and I collapsed on top of her but quickly rolled to my side. My large frame would crush her. I covered our bodies with the blanket. If we were any closer, we would be one body, one soul. She curled her body up against mine, and as her breathing began to slow, I ran my hands up and down her spine. I loved her skin. I loved everything about her, but there was more to discover.

We had been apart for more than ten years, and we had a lot to discuss. One thing was certain, I would move heaven and earth to keep her here with me and never allow anyone to come between or hurt us ever again.

TWELVE

Was it a Dream?

Shaena

W hen my eyes opened, I was in a room filled with dozens of roses, mainly purple. Large bouquets were situated on each side of Seamus's bed. *Seamus's bed?* I sat up against the headboard and nervously scanned the room. I was alone, naked and covered only under a thin sheet. I could still feel him with me, on me. And if that was not enough, marks of our lovemaking were evident along the insides of my thighs, only one of many areas Seamus kissed, licked, and left a love mark I would not soon forget.

I felt sexy, desired, and cherished. I had not been with anyone in a long time. It never felt right to give myself over to a man whom I did not love. I loved Seamus, I always had. How, after all of this time, was I here with him now? I picked up the single-stemmed purple rose that was lying across his pillow and breathed in the intoxicating aroma. I saw a copy of *The Vanishing Raven* on the side table and ran my fingers over the leather hardcover. The name embossed on the bottom did not read "Seamus O'Toole" but rather his pen name, Weston James, and that for some reason did not please me now that I knew his identity.

I knew his passion was writing; we talked about it many times when we were together. He wrote a magical story for me to find my way back to him. How did I not know that? He never stopped loving me. He penned his love in a book that I have loved since reading the very first page, and now the world loves him too.

A page near the end of the novel was bookmarked for me to read. I scanned the page until I found what he wanted me to understand:

"Although the beautiful raven-haired beauty, a wonderment that blessed my life for a short time, will never be too far from my heart, the fates will align for the young lovers to reunite one day, and once the soaring bird returns, all will be righted, and the ones who stood against them will succumb to the same darkness they had condemned the couple to be in."

What does this mean? To condemn and bring darkness to the ones who hurt us? Was he referring to my mother? Ultimately, she was the driving force behind our family leaving. My father still had months of work to be concluded in Ireland, but my mother had insisted we return to the United States immediately after she found me with Seamus.

I have read this book countless times and I thought I had it all figured out, but he wanted me to read this excerpt again. Why?

"What message does he want me to understand?" I said aloud to myself.

"Don't you know?"

I looked up to see Seamus holding a tray with tea, fruit, and scones.

"Why don't you explain it to me, before I form my own conclusions?"

"You disappoint me, lassie. I thought you, of all people, understood my work."

"I do, Seamus. Please do not misunderstand my question. You obviously are trying to make a point here, so why did you want me to read that excerpt?"

He placed the tray down to the bed and walked over to me. My hands were clenching the bedsheet when his eyes found mine.

"Please do not be afraid, not of me. May I touch you?" he asked quietly, hopeful.

"You may," I replied, as I lowered my hands with my body relaxing.

He did not kiss me on my lips as I expected him to do, but instead placed a chaste kiss to my forehead before pulling back.

"*The Vanishing Raven* was my roadmap back to you. You see, my love, after I had finished my time at the university, I was ready to come find you. I had several long discussions with my mum and dad, who both agreed that I should follow my heart back to you. I left on a plane the next day bound for New York."

"I was already at Brown."

"Yes, I know."

"How? Did you hire private investigators or something? We were worlds apart, yet you knew every aspect of my life and still did not come to me. I need to understand. Why?"

"Please, my love, calm yourself and listen to me. You were not hard to find, especially knowing who your father was. I began my search with him, and you were almost in reach. I do not believe your father ever expected to find me waiting for him in his office. He was shocked, to say the least, but welcomed and listened to me. I told him simply that I loved you and was here to see you. He seemed reluctant at first to share any information about you, but then he did something that surprised me."

"Seamus! You saw my father? What did he do that was so surprising?"

"He picked up the one framed photo of you that he had on his desk, and I saw remorse and a tear that lined his torn face. At that moment, I truly believed he was sorry for the part he played in our separation. He told me that at the time, he felt it was better to side with your mother and do as she asked. He was sorry for all the times he was not there for you as a father should be, and he hoped that he would get a chance to make it up to you one day. He placed your photo back to its place on his desk and scribbled your number on the back of his business card. When he handed it to me, I felt as if I had been given gold."

He continued, "Shaena, you must believe how much your father loved you, he told me so. He wished me well with you, and hoped if love had a way of finding us again, that his only child would be happy."

"My father was a good man, Seamus. I never doubted his love for me, but his work came first. My mother never appreciated what she had with my father. She only loved the lifestyle his money provided. When he died, she was cold and crueler than I ever thought was possible. Losing my father suddenly drove me to finish my education and be free of her once and for all."

"Are you?"

"Free?" I answered back. "Not entirely. I live my life away from her, but she always seems to find a way in to twist the knife a little bit more. She uses my father's death as a way to be connected to me, but I saw through her a long time ago. I still don't understand why you never came to me at Brown. My father gave you my number. Why didn't you call, write, or do something to let me know you were near?"

"Would it have made a difference to you?"

"What kind of question is that, Seamus? Of course, it would have. You coming to me would have changed my entire life. Did you change your mind? Was I too much trouble to bother?"

"What?" he retorted. "Ridiculous. I will not answer the most ludicrous question that I have ever heard. All I do and have done is for you. Unfortunately, there is more to my story."

"There always is."

"The day I visited with your father was unfortunately also the day he died. I was there, Shaena, and it was horrible. The image of your father dying in my arms will be something I will never forget for as long as I draw breath."

I began to sob.

"You were there in his last moments? What happened? You said he was happy. You said he wished you well. What happened?"

"Your mother arrived unexpectedly and was angered by my presence. Your father tried to reason with her as I made every effort to leave, but she came at me next. She warned me to stay away from you and leave you alone. She said that you had moved on with someone else. Of course, I did not believe her. She was irrational and not making any sense. Your father grabbed her arm to calm her, and they struggled. He stepped back and clutched his chest while she continued to shout out vile threats to me. He collapsed and passed out without your mother noticing. I immediately rushed to his side and felt for a pulse. It was weak. She finally called for help while I began CPR, but it was too late. He died."

He continued as he consoled me, "Your mother became unhinged and threw herself over his body. I remained behind until your father's body had been taken from his office. I was desperate to find you, but she stopped me again. This time she threatened to cut you off financially and force you to leave school. She said she would tell you that I was the reason your father was dead, that I provoked him and my actions caused his heart attack. I knew your mother was cruel, but in my wildest imaginations, I never thought she would hurt you that much."

He went on, "Don't you see, love, I could not risk doing that to you. I knew I would see you again, but I would bide my time and try again. As I left your father's office, women were crying over his loss. My heart hurt for you. I remained in New York until his funeral, where maybe I would catch a glimpse of you. You were alone in your grief. Even after everything that happened, I never once witnessed your mother touch you to give you any semblance of sympathy. I am so sorry. You will never know how sorry I was for you and for your father."

"You left the purple rose, didn't you?"

"I did."

"For me?"

"Yes."

"Even when I could not see you, I always felt you, Seamus. Even on that day, I felt a breeze cast over my skin, and you were there. There's more, right?"

"Yes, but how about you eat something first? You did faint earlier, after all. I could draw you a bath?"

"No, thank you. I need to hear all of it, no matter how much it tears my heart out."

"Shaena, you being here with me now is putting my heart back together. I love you so much."

He held my face, wanting to hear me say the words back to him, but after all, he shared with me, I was not ready to say them. I knew I had felt love for Seamus, but could I trust that what he said was the truth? I knew what the book said, and now to hear it from him was confusing me, and the feelings I had for him.

I suddenly needed space away from Seamus. The walls were closing in, and I needed air. I suffered from anxiety attacks since separating from Seamus all those years ago. My mother wanted to send me to a psychiatrist and pump me with anti-depressants for my mood swings. I was fifteen, we were supposed to have them, but it was so much deeper than teen hormones. She broke me and was happy to see me in pain.

I was still in pain. My father was dead, and Seamus was there when it happened. How did I not know any of this? Did my mother hate me that much to keep something so important like that from me?

I felt like I was going to be sick. I leaped off the bed and ran to the bathroom, holding my mouth and slamming the door behind me.

THIRTEEN

Wrecked and Reborn

Seamus

She locked the bathroom door and effectively kept me out. Have I revealed too much, too soon? She would not allow me to help her. I pounded on the door until it flew open, to see her standing there with tear-filled eyes.

"What can I do? Please, Shaena, we have come so far, please do not shut me out. If you are strong enough to hear it, I promise to tell you the rest. I am not blind. I see the way you are looking at me. I see doubt where just a short time ago there had been love in your eyes. Please allow me to tell you the rest of the story."

I was clenching my fists with such force that I thought my nails were going to pierce my palms. She had to believe me. What reason would I have to lie?

She walked from the bathroom, keeping a safe distance from me. She was clutching the robe she was wearing as a protective shield, staring down at the sheet she had dropped to the floor.

She said, "I need to go back to my room for some time alone, if you don't mind. I will call for you when I am ready."

She sounded cold, distant, and far from the woman who I had made love to. I could not leave her in this state without again reminding her of who we were and what we could have for our future.

"I know what I have just shared has wrecked you, but I swear it on the memory of your father and my parents that what I have said is the truth. I have no reason to re-write history. It is the truth, and there is so much more that you need to know if we are ever to move on from here. Please do not make any decisions until you hear the rest. I love you and shall be in the garden until you come back to me."

I left her on her own while my heart was shattering into a thousand pieces.

After I paced my study and ingested several shots of Irish whiskey, it came to me. I had the proof all along that would convince Shaena that I was telling her the truth. I rushed to my safe and collected what I had stowed away a long time ago. I found her father's business card that he gave to me on that day. He wrote a note on the back of it along with her number.

"Tell Shaena that I love her when you give her a copy of her favorite book. She will know what it means. I wish you a happy reunion."
-Maxwell Blake.

I held the proof in my hands. All I would have to do now is to wait for her to come back to me. I will present her with the last gift from her father and give her closure and acceptance about his death. I could only hope it was enough to keep her instead of driving her further away.

FOURTEEN

All I Ever Wanted and Needed, I Can Now Have

Shaena

The only proof that I was still breathing was the pinkish color of my skin from my hot shower. I was numb from Seamus's revelations about my life, and the truth that had been kept from me. What could my mother possibly gain from her actions?

Charlotte Blake did not appear to be weary from what she had done to me. Rather, it was the opposite. She traveled all throughout the year. She had her charities that provided the perfect photo-ops that kept her on top of the social scene and her name written in bold black letters on Page Six of the *New York Post*. Why would she bother with me with all she had in her life to keep her busy? She was too self-absorbed to care about my feelings and only showed interest when she wanted something. This time, I had refused her, and I had not heard from her since.

She was strange after I had mentioned Ireland. Could she have suspected that I may have wanted to find Seamus? We never talked about him, so I could not imagine he was the reason she would go quiet on me, unless she knew his identity. However, how could she? No one has, which brought me back to the beginning of my circuitous thoughts.

My stomach was in knots, and I was famished at the same time. I nibbled on a blueberry scone and finished the cold tea. My body felt better after eating, but how could I mend my heart?

After my shower, I threw on a pair of jeans and matched it with a cable knit sweater. It was chunky and warm. Thank you, Jesse, for including it! I had no desire to fuss with my long hair. It was easy to brush it out and let it air dry. It would take hours to do so because it was thick, but I needed to talk with Seamus. He must have been frantic after how I practically shoved him away and ran out from his room. Hurting Seamus was the last thing I wanted to do, but I felt suffocated and knew I needed time to think. My shower helped a bit, but nothing would be resolved until I heard the rest of Seamus's story. It would be close to midnight in New York. I wanted to hear Jesse's voice before seeking out Seamus.

I dialed my best friend's number only to get his voicemail. I simply thanked him for packing my sweater. After I disconnected the call, I felt stupid for the bullshit I had just left on his phone. I sat by the vanity table and nearly cried again. I missed my flowers. I missed Seamus. No matter what it cost me to hear his story, I had to find him.

I barreled down the stairs as if it was on fire. Connor was there with Aideen. He did not greet me with the curt tone I had now expected from him. His tense face appeared to be softer, and I suspected it was from Aideen's kindness. She had a way of connecting with people, even strangers like me. She was first to say hello, and then Connor spoke.

"Ms. Blake, I would like to apologize to you on how I behaved when we first met, and the subsequent interactions that followed. I was out of line and should have never shown you anything but respect."

He took me by surprise, nearly into silence by his admission.

"Thank you, Connor. I accept your apology, but may I ask a question first?"

"Of course you may."

"Why the hostility at all? You don't even know me, and yet you formed an opinion of me before engaging in one simple conversation."

"You are absolutely right, Ms. Blake. I was protecting Mr. James from suffering any more heartache than he already has."

"His name is Seamus, not Weston James," I said a bit defensively.

"That may be true, but I have only known him as Weston until he shared his story with me. You see, Ms. Blake, when I met your 'Seamus' he was not the man you see before you today. It took him a very long time to become what he revealed to you so honestly and openly. I will let him share the rest with you, but please know that I care a great deal for him. He is a good man with a brilliant mind and a heart that beats for you and only you. All I ask is that you give him the time he will need to share his story, which in a way is yours as well. He did not come this far to let you slip through his hands now."

"You have my word. Thank you for having his back."

"You are most welcomed, Ms. Blake, and thank you for still loving him."

"I never stopped…and it's Shaena by the way."

"Got it!"

The stuffy Connor Browne then turned to Aideen and held out his hand for her to take. He announced he was escorting her to dinner. She was beaming, holding his hand as they walked out the door. It appeared they shared something more than just working together. The universe had a funny way of showing you what you may miss the first few times. I shrugged it off and grabbed a coat and my gloves to find Seamus, praying it was not too late to make things right with him.

FIFTEEN

Giving Her Time

Seamus

fter waiting for Shaena by the greenhouse, still on edge to see if she would show up or not, I got restless. I needed to clear my head for a little while and made my way to the stables. I took my horse Spitfire out for some exercise. We rode for more than an hour, and then I treated him to a good brushing and apples to eat as his reward for not throwing me off his back. It had been ages since I went riding. I usually spent all my time in the study writing that everything else in my life ceased to exist.

"There you are," Shaena said from behind me.

I closed my eyes to listen to her soft voice. Thank you, God, for answering my prayers. She came back, and I will ask for your help to keep her with me.

She was standing behind me now and began petting Spitfire.

"Be careful. He bites."

"This teddy bear? Not this beauty. What's his name?" she asked while stroking the top of his mane.

"His name is Spitfire."

"He's handsome, and what a fitting name."

"Thank you. He seems to be quite fond of you, which is rare for him. He must really like you."

She closed her eyes for only a moment and then turned to look at me while still giving attention to my horse.

"Does his owner still like me?" she asked with uncertainty to her question.

I took her hands and held them in mine.

"He doesn't just like you; he loves you very much."

She looked relieved and pulled her hands back only to wrap them around my waist and get as close as she could. She smelled like lavender and honey. Her hair was still wet, and if I did not get her to a warmer place, she would catch pneumonia.

"Shaena, darling, please let's go inside. I just got you back. I will not risk you getting sick on me."

"I'm fine, Seamus. Please don't worry. Don't you know that's a myth?" she smiled through her light laughter.

"Myth or no myth, this is Ireland. It's cold and too cold for you and your wet head of hair."

I took off my cashmere scarf and wrapped it around her. She did not fight me and looked beautiful under the dim light she was standing under, almost angelic.

"Come. Let us go inside and find a spot in front of the fire, and we will talk."

She accepted my hand, and we said goodnight to Spitfire and made our way up the path back to the house.

"I figured hot chocolate was better than tea, and tea tastes awful with marshmallows," I said to her, serving her a cup.

"You always were willing to take a dare. You did not have to drink the Earl Grey after I added my fluffy weakness to your tea."

"I accepted the challenge and could not renege on it. However, it tasted awful."

We both laughed over our shared memory and sipped our cocoa.

I asked, "How are you feeling? Did you eat?"

"I'm better. Obviously, you know I took a shower, and the scone was delicious. Seamus, I'm not sure if I will ever be ready to hear the rest, but I know I have to, so I am going to trust my heart when it comes to you and really listen."

"Thank you for that," I said,

I took her cup and added it to the tray with mine. We held each other while lying on the pillows in front of the fire.

I started, "After I left New York, I knew you were devastated and alone, but I also knew you. With all of your mother's cruelty, I believed you would survive her. Once you completed your education, I would have another chance. I never for one moment thought of you with anyone but me. I am not sure what I would have done, but thankfully when I finally did reach out again, you were still on your own."

"Gee thanks, that's so flattering," she laughed.

"You know what I mean. The thought of anyone holding you like this is abhorrent to me. I am thankful that I am the one here with you."

"So am I, my love."

"Say it again," I said.

She turned over to look up to me and then she said, "I love you, my love. No matter what happens, I am here, and it's going to take more than a sad story to drive me away."

We kissed as if it was our first time back in the gardens where we professed our love to each other. For the first time, I knew we would find our way. We would always find our way. Love across the miles and oceans apart, we were here together right where we always were meant to be.

"I guess the biggest question you have is why my face is different, don't you?"

"The thought did cross my mind," she replied.

I let out my breath and held her as tightly as I could. This would be hard to re-live, but I had more than five years to prepare for it.

"When we first met, I only intended to keep you all to myself. It never occurred to me to include you in the other parts of my life. None of it mattered when I was with you. You were all that I saw, and I wanted you so very much. After we parted, I lost myself for a time, and then my mum said to me: *Your heart will never fail you. For now, you listen to where it is leading you and trust the spirit that grows inside of you. You had dreams before your love with this girl. Follow them and finish what you have started. There is no measure on love and how long the heart feels. But don't spend the rest of your life pining for love and not living. Seamus, you will have it again with Shaena, and if not, then it will be someone else that will be deserving of it. Take a new journey, my boy.* My mum was a very wise woman, and at the time, she was giving me this advice, I never dreamed of giving my heart to anyone but you. I believe it was her way of wishing for me to get what I was hoping for, but also protecting me if we never found each other again."

"What happened after that?"

"I finished my education, traveled to America and back, and then was lost again. I then remembered my mum's advice and began the next chapter in my life. I began to write *The Vanishing Raven*. I never knew that when I began writing the first few pages that it would serve as a beacon of hope leading home to you. I had stacks and stacks of journals, but this was my true masterpiece. After I finished reading it, I printed the pages and placed the original manuscript tied with ribbon and safely tucked it away in my chest of treasures, all reminding me of you."

"Sounds like a shrine."

"In a way it was. You were my temple, and I only wanted to worship at your feet. I would need to find you first and prove to you that we could defy the odds and be together. I was ready to try again, but before doing so, I had taken a trip with my parents. We took a trip along the finest attractions Ireland had to offer, one of them was the

Dunluce Castle on the Causeway Coast. No words could describe its beauty, and I was never more proud to be born in my homeland. Mum and dad were like newlyweds all over again. They loved each other so much. Their love inspired me on the day we met to take a chance and talk to you. When you crashed in to me, a collision I would welcome again and again, it was our beginning."

I continued, "On our way home, we were caught up in a violent storm. My mum begged my father to pull over until it passed, but my dad was too stubborn and we carried on. We never saw the truck. He hit us head on, killing my parents and nearly killing me too, but for some reason, I had survived. I spent close to a month in a coma with no memory of the crash. It slowly returned as my body recovered from the injuries I sustained, but my face had taken the worst of it. You would think with all the broken bones that I had, my face was the least of my worries. The accident left me disfigured, and even with plastic surgery, I would never look the same again."

She had tears in her eyes, all for me. By sharing my story with her, I was not looking for pity, but that's not what I saw when she looked at me. I saw love in her eyes. She held my face with her fingers grazing over my faint scars, and then she kissed me.

"A new face cannot change the man you are. It does not change this," she said as she placed her hand over my beating heart. "I love you."

"I love you, too. I will never tire of hearing it."

"Good. I have a lot to make up for. How long were you in the hospital?"

"Too long. I spent nearly a year recovering, and then more rehabilitation followed. When I finally found the courage to look in the mirror, I was not as afraid as I thought I would be. I no longer resembled my father but I always had my mother's eyes, and I felt her with me and knew I would be okay. For some reason, I survived and knew that had to count for something. Once released from the hospital, I needed to settle my parents' estate and discovered it was all left to me. My parents were wealthy, but you would never know it. We lived in a modest home surrounded by treasures of generations before me. Mum used to say every piece told a story. I could not live in our home knowing they were no longer there. I had everything boxed up and sold the house and the land. I erased every trace of my life with my parents and began again. Mum told me to follow my heart and begin my journey, so that's what I did."

"At the Barberstown Castle?"

"One of my many purchases."

"And Aideen? Was her story true?"

"It was. I had known her since I was young. She was my mother's best friend. She had spent a great deal of time with me while I was in the hospital. She helped me so much, and in a way, I had my mum again through her. I later discovered that she was a maid at the very castle I now owned. I fired her, and then re-hired her to be my personal assistant."

"And Connor? He doesn't look like the type of man you would be friends with."

"He wasn't at first. He was my physical therapist. I hated the bastard at first sight! He kicked my ass every single day until I was walking again. I took out every aggression on him, and he took every punch that I managed to land on him, which was not many. He was a good friend—my only friend—who saw me at my worst and never left my side. Once I began writing again, he acted as a liaison for me and the writing world. I kept myself hidden because the one person I wanted to see me was you. With a leap of courage—and some Irish whiskey—I self-published *The Vanishing Raven*. It became an overnight success. I did not care about the money, fame, none of it. I just wanted to write and hoped you would someday read the words that were meant for you."

"I wish I had known sooner. I would have come for you. Please tell me that you know that."

"I do. It was the hope of reuniting with you that kept me going.

After what happened in New York the first time, and then my accident, it was just hard to breathe. I lost everything in that accident. That's partly why I became so famously reclusive. But I have to believe my parents are watching over me and are the driving force behind my dreams."

"That is so beautiful, Seamus. I sometimes believe my father is watching over me. I wish I had more time with him. I think he would have been proud to watch me graduate from college."

"I know he would, love," I assured her.

"So, back to the book. After you found success with it, how did you feel about all the notoriety that came along with it?"

"I never expected my book to be anything more than what it was written for. Although no one knew Weston James, I somehow gained a legion of fans, which was quite surreal, if you think about it. It was like high school all over again: everyone wanted to be with me, and all I wanted was to spend time with you—the other reason why I was reclusive. Connor handled everything for me. I owe a great deal of my success to him. He's not a bad man."

"I see that now. He apologized earlier to me."

"That pleases me to hear that. I nearly kicked him to the curb after I heard him speak harshly to you. I shared our story with him. He was sympathetic to my dilemma but was also protective. He was there to bear witness to my darkest days and my brightest ones when I walked for the very first time on my own. I felt that if I could do that, then I could finally share our story with the world.

"I guess I understand why you didn't use your real name, but how did you choose Weston James? Don't get me wrong. It's a fabulous pen name, very sexy."

"Why, thank you, Ms. Blake. I tried to be as creative as I could."

"Tell me how you came up with it."

"You will laugh if I tell you."

"I will not. Now spill it!"

I loved how she listened to every detail of my story.

"Connor loves watching television. He enjoys the western sagas. One day, a movie was on about the famous outlaw Jesse James. To my surprise, I sat down and watched along with him. The gun that killed him was a Smith & Wesson .44 caliber revolver. Later that night, I was alone in my study and created my pen name. Wesson did not exactly flow, so I switched around a few letters and came up with Weston. I wrote a few additional names down on paper, and James was one of them. After I wrote it a few times, I decided to become Weston James, the novelist."

"I prefer Seamus, if my opinion matters at all."

"Oh, my love, it does. I will have you know that a position has opened up on my team, and I am in need of an agent. Do you happen to know where I might find one? I have very specific needs that require the utmost attention. I never repeat myself once I give direction. Am I making myself clear? Know anyone that can follow direction?"

"I might know someone that will best suit your needs, but first you should practice your tough and thorough interview process on me before I refer her."

Shaena wiggled herself free from my arms, walked, and twirled around the room. Her cheeks were rosy and flushed from sitting for so long in front of the fire. She looked young and carefree.

"Fair enough. You make valid points. First, let's discuss dress code. You can begin with losing the sweater."

She winked and tossed it over her shoulder. My girl wanted to play, and I was beyond excited to join in.

SIXTEEN

Back to Us

Seamus

"**Y**ou seem qualified, Ms. Blake, maybe too qualified for what I have in mind. How will I know you will be up to task? I can be quite demanding when I want something."

"I always deliver on point, and my employers are always left smiling."

"Show me how you make them smile. I would like to see up close how well you do your job."

"You are in for a treat, Mr. James. I am the number one agent in my office, and am very good at giving my clients personal attention to keep them coming back for more."

She was beyond intoxicating with her long black hair flowing down her naked back. After she lost the sweater, several articles of clothing followed, including her bra and panties. She was naked from the waist up with only her hair as coverage.

As she continued to perform her sexy striptease, I was barely holding on to my control. No woman had ever excited me as Shaena was doing right now. She shimmied out of her jeans, with her panties soon following. Like a professional model, she posed for me with her hands on her hips and went in for the kill by biting down on her lip. It did not take long for me to remove my clothing.

I rushed to her and lifted her from the floor. She weighed nothing. Easily placing her over my shoulder and lightly tapping her sexy derriere, I took my love to bed and said, "You're hired."

We made love throughout the night until our growling, neglected stomachs got our attention. We went down to the kitchen and made a feast of everything that wasn't tied down in the refrigerator.

Was it possible to finally feel complete after years of suffering alone without her? My beautiful girl was sound asleep beside me in *our* bed. I could watch her sleep forever. I would give her everything I had if she asked for it. This was the reunion I longed for, and now we had it. After completing a successful interview with the well-read Shaena Blake, I knew who I wanted to represent me in all areas of my life.

I was afraid to close my eyes in fear she would be gone when I awakened. It was different back then. She never had a choice, whereas now she had one. I prayed without a doubt that she would choose "us" over anything else she had in her life. I knew it sounded incredibly selfish, but it would be one request I would ask of her. We wasted too many years to not stay together now. She was talented and very good at her job. I followed her career from the beginning. She was part of a great team at Prestige. I did not wish to take anything from her, not when she lost too much already, no thanks to her mother.

I never understood how a mother could be so cold and downright evil. I would be generous to use any other word than the one that was best suited for her. All this time she could have been close with her daughter, but she chose to hurt her again and again instead of loving and treasuring the gift she had.

She shifted slightly in her sleep and reached out for me. I took her hand in mine and kissed her gently. I heard her say she loved me, the sweetest words this man had ever heard. I leaned in to return the endearment to her.

"I love you, too. Sleep, my angel."

Two dark as emerald green eyes were staring back at me. She kissed my lips passionately and told me it certainly was a good morning.

"Good morning, my love," she said.

I gave my body a deep stretch, and when she did not expect it, I pulled her on top of me. Her body perfectly aligned with mine and, not caring about how tired we were, we made love until sleep found us again.

The next time I awoke, it was past noon. I shot up from my bed when I realized I was alone. Anxiety started to take over. I had to tell myself, "Stop it. She's here." Her pillow was indented and carried Shaena's scent. I knew she was near. I calmed my heart down and my overactive mind. Once it had past, I gathered my robe and began looking for her, shouting at the top of my lungs.

"Mr. James, are you ill?"

It wasn't her. It was Aideen, who wore an expression of worry all over her face.

"Of course not! I'm fine? Can't you tell?"

She took a step back, not knowing what I would do or say next. I immediately regretted the tone I had taken with her. I closed my eyes and counted to five.

"My apologies, Aideen. I am looking for Ms. Blake. Do you know where she is?"

"I do. She asked to take Spitfire out for a ride. I had Finn assist her, and that was nearly an hour ago."

"I see. Thank you, Aideen. That will be all."

Aideen left, and I began to worry. What was she thinking taking my beast of a horse out on a ride, moreover, on her own? She's a city girl. I would deal with Finn later. I needed to find her at once before she got hurt.

I quickly dressed, forgoing the shower. I was not ready to wash her scent away yet. I made my way down to the stables, when she was just riding in. Thank god!

She casually said to me, "Good afternoon, sleepy head. It's about time you woke up. I was afraid you would miss out on this fabulous day of sunshine and rainbows just over that cloud to the right."

"You crazy girl. What possessed you to take a chance on Spitfire? He could have thrown you, and you would have been seriously hurt or forever maimed."

"Seamus, living in New York, I don't always get the opportunity to ride, but I assure you, my love, I am an accomplished rider, and I have the trophies to prove it."

My worries subsided.

"Fair enough, but I still prefer you to ride with me instead of alone and on your own."

"You looked so peaceful, and I didn't want to wake you. I needed to clear my head and take some time to think."

"What did you need to think about?" I asked her as I held out my arms to bring her down off Spitfire.

It was then that Finn appeared. My look should have said it all for him. He discreetly took the reins and quietly walked my horse back to his stall.

"Talk to me, Shaena. Why did you need time?"

"Isn't it obvious, Seamus?"

"Not to me," I said.

She let at a sigh and began walking ahead of me. This would not do at all.

"Shaena, stop!" I called out, and she turned to look at me.

"I lost you once, and it nearly destroyed me. I will not so easily allow that to happen again. Am I alone here? Talk to me before I completely lose my mind."

"I will, Seamus, if you give me a chance. You must understand that learning who you really are has changed my life. Up until a few days ago, I never dreamed of ever seeing you again. I prayed, if anything, that you were living your life happily, even going as far as hoping you had a wife and children. Now, that I know otherwise, is it fair to say that you want those things with me?"

I swallowed hard and answered, "Yes, I want it all with you. I've been waiting all this time for you, lassie."

"Okay then," she said, taking pause to breathe. "As I said, life changed. I am going in to take a shower. I would appreciate if you would please give me some time."

"Stubborn woman!" I muttered under my breath.

SEVENTEEN

Mothers are Supposed to Love, Not Harm

Shaena

After leaving him on his own for a while, I was thankful he did not follow me. He seemed skittish, as if I was going to disappear right before his eyes. I guess in a way, I couldn't blame him. He was right. I did not keep my promise of returning to him.

Although I was younger then, I was not naïve. What I felt for Seamus back then was real, even though my mother tried to convince me that I was foolish and downright stupid to believe him. It still hurt me to look back on the memory of his anguished eyes looking at me when I was screaming out from the car window.

My mother slapped me incredibly hard once we were out of sight, and I felt the sting of it for hours.

"You shut up right now, Shaena, or you will suffer a hell of lot more than just the slap I just delivered to you. Do you understand me?"

I kept looking over to my father, who was silent. Why was he not saying anything to stop her? When I did not respond, she slapped me again, making me cry out. She was gearing up to do it again when my father finally decided to intervene.

He grabbed her by the wrist and screamed, "That is enough, Charlotte. What has gotten into you? You are a mad woman."

She struggled, but my father was too strong and held her back until he grabbed the other wrist, completely restraining her now.

"Stop the car!" he called out to the driver.

Once stopped, all I imagined was Seamus catching up to us and rescuing me from this hell of a situation, but no one came. My father dragged my mother from the car and nearly slammed her against the hard metal to calm her down.

I remained where I was, too afraid to move. I had never witnessed my father ever put his hands on my mother, only to hug her, and most times she would be cold and push him away. He was not trying to hurt her, just calm her down before it got worse.

Hell! I did not see how it couldn't get worse. My heart had been completely broken. My face was on fire from her assault, and now I had to bear witness to my parents go at each other like brawlers in the street.

My father looked over to me, then back to my mother. She was screaming at him while my father remained in control and didn't rise to meet her outrageous behavior. I lowered my window an inch so I could listen.

"Hear me, Charlotte, and hear me now. If you ever lay your hands on our daughter again, I will make sure you regret it."

"Really, Maxwell? Oh please! I am shaking with fear," she sarcastically mocked him.

My father turned the tables on her. He was not backing down, and it appeared he reached his limit. He grabbed her chin and made her look at him.

"I dare you, Charlotte. Come at me again or hurt Shaena, and you will suffer consequences that will make your fucking head spin. I know

I am not father of the year. I work too much, and I am away more than I am home, but God help me, I am going to try to change that, beginning right now. I am not a fool. I know you do not love me the way I love you. Who knows if you ever did after you had to settle for your second choice? But the fact remains that we have a daughter and she needs both her parents, not a mother who makes her cry because of her jealousy."

My mother shoved him back, breaking the grasp he had on her, and she said, "Me, jealous? Of a fifteen-year-old? Oh, Maxwell, you have truly have lost your mind."

"No, for the first time I am thinking clearer than I ever have before, and you are jealous because your daughter has found love. And no matter how many times you try to dispute that fact, it will not make it less true. Now, you will apologize to Shaena and remain silent as we board our flight that will take us home...unless you would like to remain here on the side of the road like an abandoned dog."

"Fine! You won this round, Maxwell. But you will see that I was right to stop this romance when I did. You will see."

They both climbed into the back seat with me, while I stared out of the window. My mother did apologize, but it was only to appease my father. He gripped my thigh to let me know how sorry he was, and his face told me that he would try his best to make this right for me. But how could he? It was too late to repair the damage my mother caused, leaving Seamus and me with broken hearts.

"Damn you, mother! How could you do that to me?" I cried out to an empty room.

I hated to live in the past. I accepted a long time ago that I had lost Seamus the day we left Kildare. I never looked back, because it hurt too much. I could not connect with any man, no matter how great they looked on paper. The few relationships and experiences I allowed myself to have were just to pass the time. I only had room for one in my heart, and he was a world away.

These past few days had been wonderful, but where would we go from here? What would happen to me? Was I what my mother had always accused me of being: foolish? Was that what I was, just a foolish woman who loved the idea of being in love? Or was all that I am feeling undeniable love for the man Seamus was now, and not the boy I once knew?

I grabbed my cell phone and dialed my best friend. Come on, Jesse, please be there.

"Hey, about time I heard from you. How is Ireland, and the freak? Have you dazzled him with your hypnotizing eyes yet? It works every time. If I wasn't gay, I would be all over you, babe."

Leave it to Jesse to carry on without giving me any room to speak. I smiled because I loved my best friend so much for just being true to himself. He never apologized and did not have a care in the world. He would say what he was feeling and always expressed his thoughts in an energetic manner. The opinions of others did not bother him.

"Jesse!" I shouted into the phone to stop him from talking.

"What's up?"

"I need to talk, and you are the only one that can help me."

"You have my attention, go on," he said.

It was just then that I caught a glimpse of Seamus staring at me from the doorway. He was leaning up against the doorjamb, wearing a look of hurt on his rugged face. Did he hear me? God knows what was going through his mind right now.

Jesse was asking me if I was still with him until I finally responded with a little white lie.

"I just figured it out, best friend," I said over the phone. "I will match the aubergine top with the black slacks instead of the brown ones."

Jesse responded, "Wait! I packed brown slacks for you. Oh hell no! Do not wear anything brown, do you hear me?"

"I won't, I promise. Fashion crisis averted. I have to run now. I am late meeting with Weston. I'll call you soon."

"You get him, girl!" he called out as I disconnected our call. God!

I felt incredibly stupid, but at least Jesse bought it. I could not talk with him about Seamus, especially with how he was looking at me.

"Hi," I said to Seamus.

"Hi yourself."

"Look, Seamus, I am not sure what you heard, but let me…"

Before I could finish my sentence, he rushed over and took me in his arms, holding me close to him. He crushed his lips down to mine and began unbuttoning my blouse. He had me on my back quicker than I could speak another word. His strong hands were holding me down—not with force, but sensually. I welcomed his touch. I wanted all of him, and he did not hesitate to show me how much he wanted me.

After we made love, he held me in his protective arms and recited from memory a quote from a John Keats poem he used to read to me when we were younger:

I cannot exist without you—am forgetful of everything but seeing you again—my Life seems to stop there—I see no further. You have absorb'd me. I have a sensation at the present moment as though I were dissolving... I have been astonished that Men could die Martyrs for religion—I have shudder'd at it—I shudder no more—I could be martyr'd for my Religion—Love is my religion—I could die for that—I could die for you. My creed is Love and you are its only tenet—You have ravish'd me away by a Power I cannot resist.

"How did you know that I needed to hear that?" I whispered to Seamus.

"I know you. I have always known you from the very depths of your soul. I can only imagine how coming back here and seeing me again has stirred up all sorts of feelings for you, but I swear for as long as I live that all I have done up until now has been for you. I love you, Shaena, and I know you need time…but when you are in my proximity, I lose all ability to think straight. It has been a long time, too many years of being alone, and I never want to go back to that again. Do you understand?"

"I do; more than I can make you believe it. When you walked in and heard me on the phone, I got nervous. I thought you might have thought I was betraying your trust. I swear I was not. I just needed some advice from my *gay* best friend."

"For a less than a second, that's exactly what I thought, but then reasonability came back and kicked me in my ass. I know you would never knowingly hurt me. That is why I stayed and not fled, like the old me would have done, the hurt and insecure man who locked himself away when I should have been living."

"We have a lot to talk about, don't we?" I said as I leaned up on my elbow to look at him.

"Yes, my love, we do. How about we get dressed and have a real dinner for a change? And then I promise we can talk about anything you wish."

"Sounds like a plan."

Seamus left to speak with the kitchen and arrange dinner for the two of us, while I pulled the covers over my head, sighed, and talked out my thoughts.

"Breathe, Shaena, just breathe. This is going to be okay. You are finally with the man of your dreams. You are happy. He is all you have ever wanted, and now you can have him. I just need to reconcile our past before I could believe that I have a future with Seamus O'Toole. I believe it begins with my mother. My father is gone, and although he tried with his heart to make things better and to build a stronger relationship with me once we were home, it was not as it should have been. My mother maintained a strong influence over the both of us, no matter how hard my father tried and fought with her. I will speak with Seamus first, and then I will decide on how to confront my mother over all her betrayals and deceptions."

EIGHTEEN

Buried Secrets

Seamus

After I had arranged dinner, I met with Aideen and Connor. Aideen was my mother's most trusted friend, and Connor was mine. I needed their advice on how to handle a sensitive matter that involved Shaena and my own parents.

"You look good, sir. You look happy," Aideen said to me.

"I would agree with Aideen, but you know me, Weston. I try to remain impartial," Connor smirked.

I knew he was half kidding, but nonetheless, it made me laugh.

"Thank you. Thank you for all you have done to make this possible for me, and for Shaena. It was a risk, and not knowing how she would react was probably my biggest fear."

"She's not like that, sir. I knew from the moment I met her," Aideen interjected. "She has good in her, a kindness that was lost on that awful mother of hers. That poor child, to have had suffered with that woman. Oh, I wish I could give her a piece of my mind, and maybe a good hiding too. Forgive me, sir, for speaking out of line, but I am angry for her, and I wish she did not have to go through what you both did to be together now."

I said, "That's just it, I am not sure if we are together, but it is what I am hoping for. I need to tell her all of it before I can expect her to say yes to me. For far too long now, too many secrets have been kept from the both of us. They need to become known, and maybe she will find a new understanding to who her mother really was at a point in her life, and why she did what she did."

"I think you should reconsider, sir," Connor replied. "You have all you have ever desired finally here with you, and now you are so bold to risk losing it all after you fought so hard to get it? For the life of me, I will never understand you, Weston. Every time I believe I have you figured out, you reveal another side of you that is just maddening."

"Connor, I am who I am and never pretended to be otherwise. This was not my secret, but I have to bear the burden of it with the woman I love. I will not begin our new life together with lies. I will not do that to her."

Aideen said, "You are doing the right thing, Mr. James. Your father was a good man, one of the best, but he was human and made some mistakes. Your mother loved him in despite of it all, and he worked every day after that to make her happy until their last day together. They left this earth so in love, and they believed you would find your heart again. When you do tell Shaena what you know, please remember that this happened many years ago before you and your love for her ever existed. Their past is their own, and they made their penance, so please remember that before another word is spoken."

"Thank you, Aideen. You remind me so much of my mother. It is like having her here with me."

"She is here for me too. I see my best friend every time I look at her son."

Connor remained quiet, but I knew him well enough to know what he was silently telling me. He was a guarded man with trust issues. He could be exasperating at times, but I knew he cared. Now that he admitted his feelings for Aideen, he was happier, which pleased me to no end. She was a good person and deserved to be loved. Her ex-husband was a fool, but his loss was Connor's gain.

I poured myself a glass of my favorite single malt scotch and went back to that day with my parents.

"We need to talk, son."

"Dad, if this is about sex and love, then mum has covered it already, I'm good."

"Please?" he asked again. Something had shifted in my father's eyes, and I knew I would listen no matter what he had to say.

"This is hard for me, son, and I really do not know where to begin."

"Dad, you know you can tell me anything. What has you so upset?"

"Seamus, you have so much of your mother in you. You are kind, and that heart of yours is so big. It's no wonder you fell so fast for your American girl."

"I think we fell at the same time, if you want to know the truth. I'll get her back, dad. I know I will."

"I have no doubt about that, my boy, but there is something you need to know. I never dreamed of ever having this conversation with you. Even though we're your parents and you only see us as being old, we are entitled to a past, and I had one just like any other bloke."

"Okay...I get that. Dad, just tell me already. You are making me nervous."

"A long time ago, I too was in love with an American girl, or at least I thought I was."

"What about mum? Did you have an affair?"

"In a way, I did. But it was more an emotional one rather than physical. I was with your mum, and we were to be married, but I needed to finish my education first according to our parents. I spent a

summer studying at Oxford. I left your mother on her own while I was in England. This American woman was studying abroad, as I was. We met one day at a pub with mutual friends. She asked me to walk her home, and after that first night, we shared many more nights getting to know one another better. Just talking. She wanted more, more than I could give her, and that's when I knew it was time to go home, and home to your mother."

"I do not understand this at all. Why would you jeopardize your relationship with mum over a fling with a stranger? How could you hurt my mother like that? You betrayed her by even daring to look in the direction of another woman!"

"I know how this sounds, son, but I swear to you it never went beyond friendship and flirtation. You see, I had known your mum since we were young children scampering around this land carefree and happy. We knew one day we would be together and build a life with each other, but even in the best of relationships, you suffer a few bumps in the road. I got cold feet, and I was so used to the norm with your mum that this beautiful lassie excited me. She was different. She looked different. She talked different. She was unexpected and refreshing. I was in over my head and ended it before I left for home. She begged me to stay with her, to come back to America with her, but I refused her. She cried and cried until her pain turned to hate. She was justified in her anger, as I led her on and I was ashamed of my actions. I deserved the lashing she gave me. Then we never saw each other again...until one day, many years later, she walked into my office. I thought I was looking at a ghost, but she was real. Beautiful as ever, maybe even more since our university days."

I had a pain in my chest listening to my father's story. My mind drifted to Shaena and how she also came back to me many years later.

I swallowed hard and asked my father to tell me what he was struggling to say.

"Dad, who was the woman? Just say it."

"Charlotte Blake, Shaena's mother."

"No! It cannot be. Why are you doing this to me?"

"Seamus, I never thought I would see her again, and then she appeared as if she dropped from the sky. It's my fault why you were separated from Shaena."

"What are you saying?"

"I am telling you, son, that I would not yield to Charlotte's demands, so in return she threatened me. She confessed that she never stopped loving me, and believed it was fate leading us now. I guess after seeing you and the strong resemblance you had of me, she must have figured out who your father was, and her search brought her to my office. It was the biggest shock of my life, son."

"No, dad, this is—you telling me that when you were my age, you messed around on mum with the mother of the girl that I love. Because of you, that girl is gone, and I have no way of knowing when I will see her again. She is alone in the world with just that bitch she calls her mother. Her father is gone, and I am gone. Why didn't you tell me this sooner?"

"I thought she would stop. Son, she had everything a woman could want. She was married, a mother. She had wealth. So why would she want me after all of these years?"

"Don't you know, dad? You were probably the only one that ever told her no in her spoiled and self-absorbed life. You were a challenge never truly accomplished, so she got her second chance at you, but again, you refused her, leading her to destroy her daughter's happiness. Am I wrong?"

"No, you are not. I will never forget how angry she was with me."

"She said, 'Colin, if I cannot have you, then your son will not have my daughter. I will take her back to New York, and your precious son will never see her again.'"

"I told her, 'Charlotte, please listen to yourself. You would hurt your daughter to even the score with me? It has been over twenty years *since we parted in England. How could you still have feelings for me after all of this time? I love another. I always have and always will. Please go back to your husband, and we will put this unfortunate day behind us.'"*

"She didn't seem to take that well. She said, 'I don't think so, Colin. If I cannot have you, then your son cannot have my daughter. It is that simple. You will come to me, and if you stand me up, then you will have no one to blame but yourself.'"

"She slammed her way out of my office and I did not see her again. I left for home and told your mother everything. She wanted to scratch Charlotte Blake's eyes out, but I held her back. She wanted me to tell you immediately, and I was going to, son, but then the next day all hell broke loose, and she made good on her threat. You were in a state of devastation, and all I could do was be there for you and get you through it. I am so sorry that my past has hurt you."

"I'm sorry too, dad, but none of it matters now."

"Everything matters son. You just said you believed you would get her back. Please do not let what I just revealed to you change that. You love that girl, and she loves you. I can say this with complete truth be-hind my words, because it was your mum who was the one that showed me true love, even when I was not worthy of it. You go find your love, and never let her go again."

I swallowed another glass of Macallan, and then looked up to see Shaena watching me.

"Hello, my love," she said. "Do you like what you see?"

"I do. I always loved watching you."

"Yeah, I guess we tend to do that a lot with each other."

"You look pretty serious, are you okay?" she asked.

"Not sure. I guess my mood will improve or go on a downward spiral based on what I tell you next."

"Seamus?" she said as she stepped further into the room, stopping in front of me.

I pulled her in, resting my head on her waist. She leaned down to kiss my head and run her fingers through my hair.

"Whatever it is, I know we can get through it. Look how far we have come in just a few days. Talk to me, Seamus, and let's get through it."

"You are an amazing person. I knew it from the day we collided. I have never known anyone who even comes close to being as enchanting as you are."

"As much as I love the flattery, you are stalling. It will be alright, I promise."

"You won't run? No matter what I tell you?"

"I will not run. I promise you," she said.

A part of me did not want to leave it up to chance, so I had Shaena sit on my lap, where I could hold her. I began re-telling her the story about my father and her mother. As I went on, her grasp on me had tightened to the point of her nails digging into my skin. I took it all from her, and when it was too hard for her to hear anymore, the tears began falling. I caught each one, but more fell.

When I was finished with the story, she continued to cry and said nothing for the longest five minutes of my life. She did not run or even try to move from my lap. She just cried, and I let her. Her questions now had answers. It did not make me happy to know this was how Shaena got closure, but I believed what I did was right. My father felt I had a right to know about Charlotte, as I believed now with Shaena.

"My mother and your father? I did not see that coming."

"I'm so sorry, baby," I told her.

"You have nothing to be sorry for. We never had anything to do with them, but somehow we were caught up in something that took place before we were born. You were so lucky to have both your parents being so loving and supportive of you and each other. I wish I had met them."

"Me too," I said. "They would have loved you."

"That would have been nice. I never had that."

"Yes, you did, my love. Your father loved you. He just waited too long to show you."

"And my mother? Yeah, she was quite a peach then, and she still is today."

I said, "I have something for you. I'll be right back."

I lifted her off my lap and placed her in my chair.

"Stay here," I said as I quickly kissed her and went over to my safe where I left her present.

"Here, this is for you," I announced upon my return.

She scrunched her eyes together and then looked up to me.

"*Cinderella*. You are giving me a copy of *Cinderella*. Um…thank you."

"I am merely the messenger. I am giving you a copy of *Cinderella*, because that is what your father asked me to do."

I then handed her the card that her father gave me on the day he died. She was hesitant at first and then flipped it over.

"Tell Shaena that I love her when you give her a copy of her favorite book. She will know what it means. I wish you a happy reunion."
–Maxwell Blake.

"Your father loves you. I can rest easy now that I have delivered his message. He said you would know what this book means. Do you?"

"I do," she said, tears in her eyes. "When daddy could, he would read to me at night. I always asked for *Cinderella*. She was my favorite princess, and when he found the time, that is exactly how my father treated me. I used to believe that my real mother had died, and the one that I knew was just an evil imposter. I thought that if I prayed hard enough, the mother that loved me would return and the evil one would be banished away to a faraway land. I dreamed that my parents would be happy, and I would marry my prince someday. Seamus, by asking you to give this book to me and writing what he did on this card, did daddy believe we would find our way back to each other?"

"Yes, he did. I know he did, love, and I can only imagine how happy that his wish for us has come true. That is, if you want it to."

I waited for her answer, and then I saw it with her actions. She stood tall in front of me and placed my hand on her heart.

"Seamus, I had a moment earlier today when I doubted who I was in love with: the boy with curly red hair and freckles that I knew, or the man he became that was standing before me now. I did not know how to answer that question until now. You may look different, but you are the same in here." She pressed her hand to my chest. "I do not have the answers to why we spent our years apart with many miles between us, but I do not care anymore. What matters is that we are together now, and I never wish to be without you again. I love you, Seamus O'Toole. I never stopped."

"You took the words right out of my mouth. I never stopped loving you, Shaena Blake. I guess there is only one thing left to do."

I never loved her more than right at this moment. She looked so young and innocent. I opened my right drawer to my desk and found what I was looking for.

When she saw what I was holding in my hands, her beautiful green eyes sparkled. This was not what I had planned when I asked her to marry me, but we had come so far today with so much said that I could not wait a minute longer.

I slowly went down to one knee and looked up into her beautiful eyes once more. She was crying—of course, she was crying—but I had a feeling this time they were happy tears.

"Your dream came true, my princess. The man that is kneeling before you shall be your prince if you will have him. I will spend all of my days worshipping at your feet and never stop telling you or showing you how much I love you. The fairy tale you always dreamed of can be real with one simple word. Marry me, my beautiful raven-haired beauty. We will rewrite our story chapter by chapter, and you shall never be alone again for these arms will hold you, night after night, and never let you go. I love you. Will you marry me?"

I took out the one-of-a-kind ring and held it up for her. It was a natural cut, eight-carat green emerald surrounded by diamond baguettes and set in a platinum setting.

"Before I give you an answer to the most incredibly romantic proposal this girl could wish for…what name will be written on our marriage decree?"

Leave it to Shaena to flabbergast me with a question before answering. This was going to be fun, and I could not wait to call her my wife.

I told her, "Whatever makes you smile like the way you are now."

She coyly smiled and said, "I don't know if I could see myself being called Shaena James. I would like for it to read 'Shaena O'Toole.' If I can have that, then my answer is yes."

She held her hand out, and I slipped the ring onto her finger. I kissed her before standing up to take her mouth again and tangle our tongues together.

"I love you, Shaena O'Toole, and we are going to have an amazing life together."

We kissed repeatedly, until we came up for air.

"Hold your horses, Irishman. I am not Mrs. O'Toole yet," she reminded me.

I scooped her up into my arms and we danced around the room.

"Not yet. But we will soon change that. Now to bed, my love. We have to consummate our engagement."

NINETEEN

You Did What?!

Shaena

He looked at me with predatory eyes as I submitted to his every desire. We both had this insatiable need for the other. We made love throughout the night with little breaks in between.

My hand felt heavier now with the beautiful ring he slipped onto my finger. It was exquisite. I had never seen anything so beautiful before. He designed it with the color of my eyes in mind. I nearly melted after he told me that last night in bed.

The next morning, I woke before him and looked over while he slept soundly, and my heart felt complete. I took advantage of the opportunity to take in his new face. He had gone through hell, without me to help him through it. Every time I allowed my mind to remember his tragic story, I wanted to burst into tears.

His body literally broken...his face unrecognizable...his parents dead...how do you come back from all of that? I didn't think many could, but Seamus overcame every obstacle set before him, and this beautiful man was now mine. This beautiful, damaged man—now put back together again—would be my husband. I would never understand how I got to this place with him.

That fact was never in question for him, but I was ashamed to admit I had lost faith in believing in a happy conclusion to our story. I succumbed to all the seeds planted in my mind from my mother, and now, to find out she shared a connection with his father, just blew my mind. Seamus always believed in our connection. But what did I know about anything at fifteen? He knew, though, and when he crashed his way in…he stayed forever in my heart. I was sorry that it took me so long to get there. He would dismiss the thoughts I was having, telling me to never to think of them again. The past was the past, and we could do nothing to change it.

Nevertheless, how could I leave it behind when it was unfinished with my mother? I had to confront her with what I knew. I had not discussed this with Seamus yet, but she was my cross to bear in this life, and once she and I talked, she would no longer be a burden I continued to carry.

I was not just going phone her from the other side of the world and announce my engagement to the man she forced me to leave all those years ago. No, I needed to watch the color drain from her face when I told her about Seamus, and then I would say goodbye.

My vibrating phone brought me back to the now, and I quickly looked at the number to see it was Jesse calling me. Without waking Seamus, I carefully untangled myself from the sheets and tiptoed into the sitting room.

"Good morning, Jesse, how are you?"

"How am I? Are you serious right now?"

"Um…yes. Saying good morning when someone calls is the customary thing to do."

He replied, "Wow! I am impressed. You must have really rocked his world. Was it the hot lingerie I slipped into the side pocket of your suitcase, or was it your charm that got him?"

"Jesse, what did you add to your coffee this morning? You sound fucking crazy right now. I have no idea what you are talking about."

"You really don't know?"

"Know what?"

"James received an e-mail this morning from Weston James, stating he was ready to deal and will soon have an announcement to make to go public. He really didn't tell you? This guy is a freak, but who gives a shit, right? You signed him, and that's all that James cares about. Congratulations on another successful win. I am dying to hear all about it, but I have a staff meeting to attend without my girl. I miss you so much. You need to get your ass back to New York so we could celebrate. Oh, I forgot to tell you, with James in such a good mood, he asked me to meet him for lunch after the meeting today. Not that my hopes are up for anything, but it will be interesting to see what he has to say. Okay, I have to run. Love you, babe."

Our call ended, resulting in a headache for me. Jesse would not shut up for a second to allow me to get a word in. He hung up before I had the chance. I was still trying to figure out how an email was sent to James, since Seamus never left my side. I was so lost in thought when Seamus entered the sitting room.

"Are you okay, love? Why are you out here all by yourself?"

I looked over to him to see worry in his eyes. I did not want to begin our new life together in a quarrel, but I had to ask him about the e-mail.

"I just got off the phone with my friend, Jesse. You remember me telling you about him. He works with me at Prestige. He just finished telling me how excited our boss was this morning after he received a letter of intent from you. Tell me something, Mr. James, just what contract do you intend to have with me?"

I could not help the sarcastic tone to my voice, but it just felt like I had been duped. I wanted to smack myself for even thinking that, but last night was about Seamus and me, not some fucking book deal.

"I'm *Mr. James* now? Last night I was Seamus. I should know since, you screamed my name every time you came. You're upset, darling. Please tell me why."

"Seamus, explain the e-mail, and then I will tell you why I'm upset."

"At least we are back to calling me Seamus. We will begin there. Actually, no, we will begin with you showing me a smile. Tell me how much you love me, and then put your arms around me."

"I love you," I said as I cradled myself on his lap, where he wrapped his arms around me.

His scent was already igniting my arousal that I needed to squeeze my thighs together. His hair was all tousled on top of his head, and his beard was rough to my soft skin. How could I be angry with him for a second when all I wanted to do was ask him to make love to me?

"I guess two out of three requests are better than having nothing at all. Oh, Shaena, my love, don't be angry with me. As for the e-mail, yes, it was sent to your boss in good faith. I had scheduled that letter to send over to him regardless what happened with us. I would not damage your career just because it did not work out how I dreamed it. Lucky for me, I got the girl, and your boss got the deal he has always wanted."

I said, "You make it sound so simple. Seamus, we have not discussed anything beyond last night. Signing you as a client was the last thing on my mind. How could you believe I even cared about that after the days and nights we shared?"

"For the hardcore badass you claim to be in the literary world, it is not evident right now. Think about it for a minute. Today was your deadline. If your boss had not received a confirmation from you by the start of business hours this morning, New York time, the outcome for you would not have been good. Whatever friendship you believe you have with him would have meant nothing if you did not return with a contract in hand. This business is cutthroat and not willing to hand out second chances. He would have not been kind. I have worked with many men like James. At the end of the day, it comes down to business. Don't believe your friendship with him trumps his desire for success."

"That's a strong judgment of someone you haven't met."

He replied, "It's the reality of the business, nothing more."

"So, are you saying you are ready to come out to the world you have been carefully hiding from since your first book? Your readers want to see you. They need a deeper connection to you than just your words. They want the pictures. They need the interaction with you and want to believe it is not a publicist or assistant chatting with them. They want you."

"They will have me, but as far as 'coming out' as you say, my answer is no. I do not wish to do signings or find myself caught up in the bottomless pit of social media. Trust when I say this: James will yield to my every request, or he will not have me as a client."

"It's that simple, you say?"

"Yes, it is. You should know better than anyone how I never give up nor do I like the word 'no.' Look, Shaena, by sending the letter of intent to him, it completes the task you were given. Now, it is up to higher management to agree to the terms. He may get his feathers ruffled a bit, but he will not say no to me. I'm too much in demand."

"Yeah, I've heard that about you," I said, giggling quietly into the crook of his neck.

He loved when my breath was on his skin. I might as well light a match to ignite Seamus. He carried me back to his bed, made sweet love to me, and promised me that all would be okay. All I had to do was trust him. I did with every fiber of my being.

As we sat down for a late breakfast in the atrium that looked out to the many gardens the Barberstown Castle had to offer, Seamus handed me a thick envelope.

"This is the contract. Once you approve it, I will have Connor send it over to James."

I opened the envelope and began flipping through the beginning pages. It was ironclad including a non-disclosure agreement. His privacy to be handled with the utmost discretion, and if his needs were not met, it would immediately result in termination of the contract.

"You have thought of everything," I said as I placed it down.

"I have. This is what works for me. I gave it some thought, and I am happy knowing that *you* know who is truly writing the words behind the penname. I am Seamus O'Toole to you, but to the rest of the world, I am Weston James."

"Oh, baby, how do you separate the two?"

"Shaena, the writing was always about you. I never dreamed it would be anything else. I will always honor my parents by keeping their name. In truth, the only time I ever felt like the man I was before my accident was when I was with you. If I never write another word again, I will be okay with that. My reason for everything I do in this life is for you. You are the beacon that guides me, and wherever you want me to go, I will."

"I don't want to share you with the world," I admitted.

"You don't have to, baby. You have all of me, and I have you. That is all we need. No one ever has to know that Seamus O'Toole and Weston James are one and the same. I am not the first writer to write under an alias, and I am sure that I will not be the last."

"I understand that, but to never reveal yourself at all is complicated."

"Not to me, and it should not be for you. I like it this way, and to have complete control over my career gives me peace. I could walk away from this at any time and would be completely okay with it. I just want to love and marry you."

"I'm still pinching myself to wake up from this magical dream. How will I ever explain to my friends back in New York that I'm getting married and moving to Ireland? Jesse is going to pitch a fit of hysterics once I tell him my news."

"You would do that for me?" he asked.

"Do what?"

"You would move here to Ireland to be with me? To live here with me?"

"Seamus, I believe that when I said yes to marry you, I would assume living with my husband would be one of the perks I get to enjoy. Do you want a long distance marriage? I cannot see any fun in having that."

"Of course not! I want you with me always. I guess I am the one pinching myself now, believing you will soon be my wife and return to Kildare to share the life we were destined to have. I love you so much!"

I asked, "Will you go back to New York with me? I have to talk to Jesse, and then there's my mother to deal with."

"Try to stop me, but, my love, just because you are changing your address doesn't mean I expect you to change your life. You have a thriving career you worked very hard to achieve. If your boss is smart, and I believe he is, then he will allow you to remain with Prestige. You can just do your job from Ireland."

"As wonderful as that sounds, my job also requires a lot of traveling, and I am not excited to leave you so soon. I work long hours, and I don't want to begin our marriage with me being the absent wife. I love what I do, and I could do it anywhere, but it would have to work for the needs of my family. Right now, it fits for the single person with no life. But you changed all of that in a matter of a week. I cannot ever return to the life I had before I boarded the plane to make my return to Kildare."

"When you say 'family,' am I to assume that includes children?"

"Absolutely. I want babies with you, Seamus, and soon. All boys with dark curly red hair with just a touch of freckles."

He was happy, but I sensed sadness too.

"Hey, where did you just go?" I asked.

"I want babies with you, too. But every once in a while, my mind goes back to the accident, to the day the doctor removed my bandages, and I did not look like my father. A stranger was looking back at me. My own children will not look like me."

"You are still you. You are the one that I love, and most of all, you are still Colin and Mary O'Toole's son. You will always be their son."

"Thank you, love. Thank you."

I took him in my arms and held him, kissing him softly. He said my return brought him back to life, but that's not what I believed. It was Seamus's faith and the love that never faltered. He had gone to hell and back to regain who he was. His sheer will and perseverance got him here. He could give me all the credit, but it was Seamus who pieced himself back together. And he did that for me too.

TWENTY

Facing the Devil, One More Time

Seamus

I left Shaena on her own for the next few hours so she could make calls to her boss and best friend. Aideen was helping her pack, but Shaena surprised me with telling Aideen to instead move her things to my room. If my heart had the power to burst with the abundance of joy I felt, that was the moment to do so. I finally had all that I ever wanted, and this was real, I repeated over in my mind.

I intended for our trip back to the states to be swift and with no issues. If her mother dared to make her spill one tear, I would make certain that she regretted it for the rest of her life.

Shaena was determined to see her no matter how much I objected to it. She told me she would not be able to move on until she got closure. I could not blame Shaena for wanting it, as I had years to come to terms with all of this. But she only learned of her mother's deception a few days ago. I tied up some loose ends on my desk, and then Connor arrived to go over my itinerary for our trip.

"I just passed Ms. Blake's room. She was laughing with Aideen. They seem to have become fast friends."

"Yes, they have. It pleases me to know she has a friend in Aideen. Her mother is a travesty. I will say I am not exactly jumping at the fact I will soon see Charlotte Blake again. I was hoping our last encounter would be my last, but this trip is for Shaena. I will take pleasure in announcing our upcoming nuptials to her beastly mother. Her look alone will be priceless. My father dodged a bullet there by not getting intimate with that python. She would have choked the life out of him, just like she nearly did with her daughter."

"She sounds delightful," Connor smirked.

"That's one word I would not use in describing Charlotte Blake. I do not wish to remain in New York any longer than I have to. I am looking forward to meeting James Gentry. Shaena was quick to defend him when I questioned their friendship."

"Sir, you have not changed your mind about your privacy, have you?"

"I have not. I will be Seamus to him, Shaena's soon-to-be-husband. The mystery of Weston James will remain intact.".

TWENTY-ONE

New Beginnings Begin with Closure

Shaena

Seamus was relentless on my body as he took me over and over again until I could no longer form complete sentences. We had a lot to make up for, he kept repeating as he kissed and marked me. Hours of endless pleasure had my body and mind well-sated for our cross Atlantic flight back to New York.

I wasn't about to complain, but I was worried about seeing my mother again. Her manipulations played a huge role in changing my life and Seamus's. Charlotte Blake would answer my questions even if I had to pull out her perfectly set hair strand by strand.

I looked over to Seamus, who was sleeping with his hands crossed over his broad chest. He was a sight to take in. He told me there was a time after his accident how he felt about his disfigured face. He referenced the tale of *Beauty and the Beast*, and he was the beast. He was wrong, so wrong. Although, now that I think about it, when we met, Seamus would read me pages of poetry where beauty never factored in but it was the feeling between the two lovers that counted. Regardless, whatever age he was and whatever face he had, he was devastatingly handsome to me, inside and out.

Seamus grabbed hold of my fragile heart when I was fifteen, and he never left. I lived my life with the utmost certainty we would never reunite, but here we were and engaged. How was this my life? I was afraid I was going to wake from this magical fantasy and my mother would be there by my bedside laughing at me and telling me, "I told you so! Believing in love is for suckers and you're the biggest one!"

"Hey, what are you thinking about?" Seamus said, interrupting my thoughts.

"You."

"Oh, my love, you don't lie well. Come up here and talk to me."

"I'm worried."

"About?"

"My mother. Seamus, she is going to freak out and not in a good way. I understand her now, because I know what drove her to this level of hatred. She didn't get her way with your father, so she does not want me to be happy with his son. I just got you back. I will not risk our love again by bringing you face-to-face with the person responsible for tearing us apart."

"I am not worried and neither should you. Your mother can no longer hurt us, and believe me when I say that I have been waiting a long time to put her in her place."

"Like you wrote in your book? You speak of condemning the one who hurt us to darkness. Is it my mother who you are referring to?"

He deeply sighed and ran his fingers through his thick mane of hair. I hated to bring back these memories, but I needed to know how far Seamus's need for retribution would go.

"Shaena, we have been over this, I explained my reasons to you."

"I know, but I need to hear them again. If my mother can no longer hurt us, then why should she be condemned to darkness? We are in the light now, Seamus, and she can never break through that. Our love is too powerful and strong for anyone to ever attempt to break us again."

"My love, I will not hurt your mother, nor will I let her hurt you. The reference to darkness is simple. Her heart is cold and filled with malice. If she chooses not to accept the beautiful gift she has in you, then, my love, I fear she will be lost. Your mother will be lost, and no matter how hard you try to bring her back, she will be gone. Her list of sins is long. She has never asked for forgiveness, because she believes she was right in her actions. You're right. This trip may be wasted on her, but not for us. You have turmoil deep inside of you which needs to be gone. The only way that will happen is finally confronting what put it there, and then we will banish it and never think of it again."

"To darkness?" I asked.

"It will be her choice, not ours."

I was cold to the point of shivering. I hated to think of my mother that way, but what Seamus said was true. I had always felt it, but she was my mother, and mothers were supposed to love and protect their children, not hurt them. Seamus wrapped his arms around me and held me close to him. He was wearing a thick cable knit sweater that felt like a warm blanket on a cold night. He had protected me all of these years even when I didn't know it. He would be my strength when I talked to my mother. I would not weaken under her coldness.

If I ever needed my father, this was the time. I missed him so much. People cannot control who they fall in love with, no matter how hard they tried. He loved my mother, even at the lowest moments when she could not return his love and loved another. I said a silent prayer for my father, and though she may not have deserved it, one for my mother too. One does not know where to go unless shown the way. Maybe my prayer would help her.

With such heavy thoughts on my mind, the trip back home was so quick and such a blur.

"Nice place," Seamus said as he carried in our bags through my apartment.

"Thank you, I kind of love it. The roommate thing never worked out for me, so after a few not so great places, I found this one."

"How long have you lived here?"

"Too long and very alone. Thank goodness for Jesse, or I would have lost my mind. By the way, he lives upstairs."

Although I shared some facts about my friendship with Jesse and the fact he is gay and in love with our boss, the look in my lover's eyes were of the green-eyed monster. Okay, so maybe he did have a little beast in him, but it made my insides heat.

"Will we be expecting him anytime soon?" he asked.

I tried not to smile too brightly, because with Jesse having a key to my apartment, anything was possible.

"I don't believe so. It's late, and he doesn't know I was coming home tonight."

"Good, I'm not in the mood for any surprises when we are deeply enthralled in our lovemaking."

"You seem pretty sure of yourself. What if I'm too tired for that?"

"Are you?" he asked.

"I'm not, and I was just teasing you. The bedroom is that way."

Our little game was over for now and Seamus did not waste another minute making his intentions known. He carried me off to my room and locked the door for safe measure.

"Close your eyes, my love."

His voice was hypnotic, pulling me deeper and deeper into a haze of desire. He slowly removed me from my clothing and left me bare and on display for him. I wanted to open my eyes, but he asked me to keep them closed. Strong hands caressed my face and worked their way down my neck, across my breasts, and down to my dripping core. My hands were held in place beneath his, as Seamus took my pussy into his mouth. He sucked and lapped up my juices as he made me come so fucking hard. My eyes were closed, and I thought I saw stars dancing over my head.

I had never felt so high in all of my life and was completely drunk on Seamus. I wanted to return the favor, but I could not move if I wanted to. He parted my legs with his knee and entered me with the skill of a perfect lover. He finally released my hands, so I could touch him. We were connected in every way possible.

He commanded me to look at him, and when I did, he said, "I love you. The Raven has returned, and I shall never let you go again."

My arms encased his body, and I knew I was home.

"Time to wake up," was all I heard a few hours later, when my body was bouncing up and down with a very overgrown child jumping all around my bed.

"What the hell, Jesse! How are you in my apartment?"

Oh my god! I nearly knocked out my best friend from my bed as my eyes scanned my bedroom. My heart was beating rapidly from my chest, and it actually hurt.

"Where is he? Where's Seamus?" My hand covered my heart as I tried to calm down. "It was a dream. Oh my goodness, it was a dream."

Jesse plopped down beside me and said, "Okay, Shae, you are scaring me. You need to talk to me and tell me what has you so freaked out."

"It was a dream! None of it happened, Jesse. Seamus…"

"Who the hell is Seamus?"

Before I could answer Jesse, my tears were falling and blinding my eyes to where I could not focus anymore on my friend, who was now shaking me. Did I pass out? Then I heard his voice.

"If you like having arms, it would be best to release Shaena at once."

"Seamus!" I screamed, as I practically leaped out from Jesse's hold, out of bed, and into his strong arms. "You're here. I didn't dream it, right?"

"Oh, baby, of course you didn't. I was out getting breakfast, after taking in the scraps you had in your refrigerator. You don't go in there much, do you?"

I wanted to laugh, but I still had some tears left to fall.

Seamus said to me, "I told you last night that I was never letting you go. We are real, my love, we always were. Now, dry those tears, and let me hold you and give you a proper good morning greeting."

Ignoring Jesse, Seamus did what he promised and crushed his mouth down to mine. When I finally came up for air, Jesse was beside himself.

"Um...hello. Care to introduce me to your friend?"

Jesse glared at me and shot a dagger or two at Seamus, who was just enjoying this a bit too much. My man was jealous, and it was as clear as if it was written in neon lights.

"I am Seamus O'Toole, and I am this beauty's fiancé."

"No way! Get the fuck out of here."

"That's exactly what I should be saying to you. Why are you still here?" Seamus retorted.

"Okay, boys," I said, "back to your neutral corners. Jesse, before you ask, it's true. Do you remember before I left, I shared with you a story about having a 'once in a lifetime'?"

"Yeah, I remember."

"Well, this is him," I whispered as I took Seamus's hand.

TWENTY-TWO

Believe It

Seamus

S o this was the best friend who I had heard so much about. He got
to have a key to her place. He got to lay in bed with her and dry
her tears when she cried. He had been filling a role that should
have been mine from the beginning.

"Let's begin again, shall we?" I asked Jesse.

I extended my free hand out to him and re-introduced myself to
him as Seamus O'Toole. He shook back but still was looking at Shaena
and then to me.

"I'm sorry. I may need a minute to catch up here. I sent my best
friend off to Ireland, and without any word to me at all, she returns
home with a fiancé. Excuse me, but I think I need a little bit more information before you and I become friends."

Shaena intervened, "Jesse, it is a long and complicated story. I am
still trying to catch up myself, and I'm sorry if I freaked you out earlier
when you woke me up. Everything lately has been so perfect, and I've

been so afraid that the past days have been all a dream. So when I woke up and found you here instead of Seamus, I believed it."

"I'm here, love, and I am very real," I told her.

"I know that now, you jerk," she said. "Next time, wait for me to wake before leaving, okay?"

"Always," I replied. "I really was only trying to surprise you with breakfast in bed. Do you forgive me?"

My hands were caressing her back in slow motion, as she was falling under my simple art of seduction. With just my eyes looking into hers, she was completely captivated.

"Still with me love?" I asked.

"For the rest of my life..." she whispered.

TWENTY-THREE

The Other Guy in My Life

Shaena

I hugged Seamus again and then turned back to my friend, who was still in shock. I was especially thankful that I had clothes on. Gay or not, explaining how Jesse was in my bed while I was naked would not have been a great way to begin our morning.

"Can we all talk over some coffee?" I asked.

They both smiled, and we went into the kitchen. The breakfast Seamus had gotten for us turned cold, so I made a fresh pot of coffee. As empty as my fridge was, this I always had on hand and never ran out of.

"I guess Ireland was not only good in securing Weston James, but you come back all shiny with a fiancé on your arm. You never cease to surprise me, sunshine, but this one takes the cake," Jesse winked as he sipped his coffee. "Okay, while we're still young, share the sappy shit with me."

"You do have a way with words, my friend," I told him.

"Would you rather me be anything other than myself?"

"Not a chance," I said. "Okay, will you settle for a chapter now? And the rest of the book details later?"

"If you must."

Seamus took the hint and gave me a few minutes alone with my best friend. He kissed me tenderly and told me he loved me. I had an office in my apartment where Seamus discreetly retreated to until I was finished talking with Jesse.

"Lucy…you have some 'splaining to do," he said.

I had to hold by stomach on the account of the happy reminder of our favorite past time. When we first moved into our building, Jesse and I binged watched every *I Love Lucy* episode over one weekend. We overloaded on junk food and commiserated together about how sucky our love lives were. I looked up, knowing he knew where my mind went back to.

"I love you, BFF," I told him.

"Yeah, I know."

"Before all sorts of crazy run through your mind, please know that I am perfectly sane. Seamus was someone who I met when I was fifteen while temporarily living in Ireland. We met. We fell in love. We parted and never knew if we would ever reunite. Anyway, you know how fairy tales go…there is always a villain. That role was played by my beloved mother, who happened to know Seamus's father years prior when they were at school together."

"What? Wow! My head is spinning."

"Mine too. Anyway, when given the opportunity to return to Kildare for Prestige, all thoughts of Seamus flooded my heart, as if he never left."

This was where I needed to be careful with Jesse and not give away Seamus's identity and expose him as Weston James.

I continued, "After meeting with Weston and dazzling him with why he should be with Prestige, I had time on my hands to take some 'me' time. And that's when my path crossed with Seamus again."

"Where? How did you meet again?"

Jesse looked happy for me. He wanted every detail and waited patiently for them. Jesse believed in romance and yearned to have one of his own with James.

"I took an afternoon to visit my favorite garden, and I turned and he was there. It was as if the clouds had parted and the sun shined down on the two of us. The years spent apart from the other had just vanished, and all we had was the now. I know it sounds crazy, but the truth could not be any more real than at that moment we reunited. I've loved him since I was fifteen, a 'once in a lifetime.'"

"Wow, this is the sappy shit that writers make millions off of. Does this guy write? Because if he does, you really have to be his agent."

If Jesse only knew.

"You look happy, probably the happiest I have ever seen you. No, maybe not that happy. There was that one time when you crushed Stapleton's balls when you landed Chance Connors instead of him."

"Yeah, that was a good day," I said, giggling.

We laughed and talked for another hour before I asked Seamus to join us. We missed breakfast and ended up ordering Chinese food for lunch. After the thaw defrosted, Seamus and Jesse found a common ground. They talked and got to know one another. They needed to be friends, because Jesse was a big deal in my life, and I was not letting him go.

"Well, kids, it's been fun. I've ignored my cell phone all day, and I guess I should call James."

"He must be on the warpath by now with the two of us not in the office."

"Nah, no worries. He is still high over the coup over Weston James. The door attendant gave you up, and then I slipped and texted James that you were back. He freaked but in a good way, and he wanted me to retrieve the contract and get you in the office. James could wait. Finding you so happy takes precedence over any work deal."

"Thank you, Jesse. Are things any better with James? On our last phone call, you were pretty excited."

"We are the same. I guess it was just the euphoric feeling over Weston. James and I met for drinks and went back to his apartment, where I fell hopelessly at his feet. We had a moment, and then I rushed it, resulting in James pulling away from me…again. I'm happy for you, Shae, I really am, but I don't really see any happy endings in my future with James."

"I'm sorry."

"Yeah, me too, but that's the last thing I want to hear from you."

"Jesse, please don't give up. You never know. Look at me, I'm the living proof of the romance cliché of happily ever after's."

"I'll keep that in mind."

I hugged him with all that I had, willing him not to give up on love. I was the non-believer in the relationship, where Jesse never stopped chasing his heart. He loved James, and I knew James loved him. They just needed to get on the same page.

"I have to run. It was very nice to meet you, Seamus. You have an amazing girl here. If you're smart—which I believe you are—then cherish her forever and never take her for granted. You two have another chance to make it right, so don't fucking blow it."

"You have my word. Shaena will always be treated like the princess she is."

"Good, because I would hate to kick your Irish ass."

I laughed and Seamus did too.

"Thank you, my love," I said to Seamus, who kissed me passionately after Jesse departed.

He said, "I will admit, I like your friend, but I will also admit how much I did not like seeing him in your bed. Every trigger I possess went off like a sounding alarm. I didn't like it. I will ask you to not have that happen again, if only for my fragile heart I must protect, or I may have to kick his ass."

"Seamus, you have to understand my relationship with Jesse. He's not only my best friend, but I look to him as a brother. I don't have many real friends in the work that I do, and that number is even smaller in my personal life. But I do have Jesse, and he has been the only person I could truly count on for anything I ever needed."

"I'm sorry I wasn't there when I should have been. You lost your father, and you practically have no mother, but in name only."

"Please never apologize to me. You have been through so much these last years too, and you went through it all alone. You lost so much more than I ever did, and it breaks my heart that I was not there for you," I said.

I did not want to cry, but looking in his eyes, it was so hard not to. Seamus wrapped his arms around me and kissed the top of my head. He held me in place as we breathed the other in. I felt loved and safe, a feeling I hadn't known for a very long time. He brushed my hair out from my eyes and kissed me again.

He said to me, "I think we both have had our share of losses and grief. My parents loved me with all of their heart, and I know it would have hurt them to know I was not living my life as it was destined to be. Through losing my family to the pain I endured in my accident, I fought my way back to you. No one could ever have the power to separate us again. I see the worry in your eyes for what lies ahead for you tomorrow, but you need not to be afraid. We will face your mother together and share our happy news with her. Anything that happens after that will solely be on your mother."

"I love you, Seamus. Thank you for not giving up on me."

"I love you, too. Let me make love to you and show you how strong our love is."

I nestled my face in his warmth and gave him my answer.

"The bedroom is that way," I winked.

"I remember the way, lassie. Thank you for the reminder."

Not a second later, I was in his arms and was carried off to our private bubble. He would always protect me and keep me safe from anyone who could hurt us.

TWENTY-FOUR

Lost Soul

Seamus

My beautiful girl tossed and turned throughout the night instead of finding comfort in my arms. She had a nightmare, a brutal one. She said it was always the same one playing on repeat in her mind. Even in moments of bliss, the nightmare only returned when she was afraid of more loss. It brought her back to the most painful time in her life, when we parted. She shared with me how even in her sleep; she would have to cover her ears to prevent hearing the maniacal tone to her mother's laughter. It was as if her mother got pleasure from seeing her daughter in pain.

It was dawn when I had about enough. My patience had run out, and I wanted to punch something and really hard. I hated Charlotte Blake for just existing. She was cruel and did not know of love.

Knowing I could not hit my intended target, I kissed my love, left her a note in case she woke up, and went for the longest run of my life. I thought back to my conversations with my father, and even then, I didn't believe Charlotte understood what real feelings were. What she felt for my father was lust, infatuation, and a need to conquer. When he denied her, then she raised the stakes, and years later, her daughter paid the price. I paid the price.

Now, after all this time, and in just a couple of hours I would be laying eyes on her again. If I could and knew it would not hurt Shaena, then I would have a private plane on standby to take us home to Ireland, but my girl still had her boss to deal with and then say goodbye to her friend. These two things I knew would be difficult for her, but she chose me, and by doing so, she promised to begin her new life with me when we made our return to Kildare.

After a hot shower, I threw on a pair of sweats, hoping to climb back into bed with her, but Shaena was sitting up and looking wide awake.

"Good morning, my love, have you slept at all?" I asked as I made my way over to her.

"I'm sorry, Seamus."

"For?"

"Do you want the list? It seems that all I do is apologize, and I am afraid I am hurting you. Are you sure I'm worth the trouble?"

She wrung out her fingers with her head down. This was her mother's doubt creeping back in and manipulating the hell out of her.

"Is that a serious question? Because if you say yes, then I may need to take you to the hospital for an examination. Listen to me for the last time. You are amazing. You are beautiful. You are smart. I'm not sure how this beauty with hair of the color of night found a place in my heart and stayed, but you did, and it forever changed me. You have beautiful gifts that make up who you are. I know what this is about, and I want you to stop these self-deprecating thoughts right now. We do not have to see her today or any day after that. I will protect you always. You hardly slept last night, and it broke my heart to watch you in such distress. She cannot hurt you anymore, please know that."

I held her arms and made her look at me when she tried to turn away.

I said, "I'm here, Shaena. Let me in, and shut her out."

"I'm trying, Seamus, but it's hard."

"You must try harder, because if you don't, then we will not stand a chance at making it, and I told you back in Ireland how I felt about that. I will move heaven and earth to never feel the way we felt the day you left me. Now, dry your eyes, and go get ready."

"Yes, sir, bossy man. It's kind of hot."

"That's good to know because I am bossy, and you have to the count of five to get this lovely and very delectable derriere in the shower."

"Join me."

"Stop it, you mad woman. If I join you in there, then we are not going to end up anywhere today."

"I really am seeing my mother today, aren't I?"

"Afraid so. That is, if you haven't changed your mind."

"Of course I have, like a thousand times, but I need to pull the Band-Aid off."

"That's my girl. Go get ready. I have to make some calls, and then we can go."

She kissed me and practically skipped off into her bathroom. I saw the light in Shaena's eyes just now. It was a wonderment to take in. Her mother would feel my wrath if she dared to hurt her today.

I phoned Connor to make sure all was in place for my visit today with Charlotte Blake. I had taken measures to ensure the New York socialite would reap what she sowed if she hurt my beautiful girl again.

"When should we expect you back in Ireland, sir?"

"Hopefully the day after tomorrow. I do not wish to remain in this city any longer than I have to. We are meeting Gentry tonight, and then Shaena will meet with him tomorrow on Weston James's behalf. I will remind Shaena to conference you in when it comes time."

"Will do, sir. Good luck today."

"Thank you, Connor, but I am not the one that will need the luck."

"I'm ready," my angelic beauty said from behind me.

I turned around to see my raven-haired beauty looking stunning.

I told her, "I do love women in skirts, especially my woman. Damn, darling, you are wearing that skirt as if it is a second skin. Come here…now. You look beautiful."

"Thank you. Are you sure it's not too tight?"

"It is extremely tight, but all in the right places, and if your heels were any higher, I would be looking up to you."

"Let's get this over with, darling, and then you can take me to meet the illustrious James Gentry."

"I think that's how he would describe you, my love."

"Well, he's not meeting Weston James. He is meeting your fiancé."

"That he is."

We arrived in front of the Barberry Hotel in just under twenty minutes. She had decided not to give her mother any opportunity to reject to our visit. Shaena wanted the element of surprise, and introducing a fiancé would do just nicely. My girl was quiet, but showing no signs of apprehension. Our all-night romp in bed was just what we both needed to get through this morning with her mother.

We took the elevator up to the twenty-eighth floor to where her grandiose apartment was located. She rang the bell and took a step back to take a breath. My hand was on the small of her back, keeping her calm and in place.

"You can do this," I assured her.

"I know. Just stay by my side, okay?"

"Always."

The door opened.

"Hello, Charles, I am here to see my mother."

The older man smiled warmly at my girl and then took her in his arms for a hug.

"You look good, Charles. I trust she is not working you too hard these days?"

"All is under control, Shaena. I think she keeps me around for antique value. Come, let me show you to the living room for tea."

We took a seat beside each other while we waited for the queen to make her grand entrance. My girl's knee was bobbing up and down so furiously that I needed to place my hand on it to calm her.

"Breathe, darling, just breathe," I said to Shaena as Charlotte called out.

"Charles, I do not appreciate to be summoned and…What are you doing here? I assumed you were still in Ireland. You know you missed the foundation ball. I do hope whatever you were doing over in Kildare was worth disappointing your father."

Bitch! I was screaming in my head. This woman never seemed to change. No, I'm wrong—she's worse.

"Always a pleasure seeing you, mother, and when you are so chipper in the morning. As for disappointing daddy, I really don't think I have to worry about that anymore on the account that he is dead. Secondly, my work is important, not that it ever mattered to you. Thirdly, I am not here to discuss any of those talking points right now. I have other matters that we need to discuss and, by all accounts, are long overdue."

"I beg to differ, my daughter. You should have called and made an appointment, as everyone else seems to do. See Charles for an available date."

"I don't think so, mother. I am not everyone else. I am your daughter, and you will see me, and you will certainly hear me."

"Oh, really? And just how are you going to stop me from walking out of this room?"

"Like this."

Shaena grabbed her mother and gave her a shove to the sofa, where she bounced up and down for a second. Charlotte never saw it coming. *Priceless.*

"Shaena! What has gotten into you? You strong-arm me like a street thug. How dare you!"

"No, mother, how dare you. Do you not even see that we are not alone here? Have you gone blind not to notice that there is someone other than us in the room? Now, show me that you have some sense of manners within you somewhere, and say hello."

"And to whom am I saying hello to?"

Shaena took my hand, gave me a smile that beat all smiles before it, and walked me over to Charlotte.

"Mother, I would like for you to meet my fiancé, Seamus O'Toole. Seamus, I believe you already know my mother, Charlotte Blake."

"Hello, Mrs. Blake, you are just as I remember you to be."

As I brought her hand to my lips, I whispered to Charlotte where Shaena could not hear me, "Close your mouth. You wouldn't want to catch flies now, would you?"

She shot daggers at me with her cold eyes, and I knew I had her attention.

"Forgive me, Mr. O'Toole, but how are you suddenly my daughter's fiancé, considering that when she left for Ireland, she was single?"

"It's a great story, but I think I will allow Shaena to tell you. Love? Will you be okay here on your own with your monster—I mean, your mother?"

"We will be fine," she said as she winked at me.

I took that as a good sign that she had everything under control.

TWENTY-FIVE

Why Did You Do It?

Shaena

"**N**othing to say, mother? I would have thought you would have plenty."

"What would you like me to do? After all that I did to prevent this moment from happening, here you stand, engaged. Why, Shaena? Why do you defy me at every single turn? That man was never good enough for you then and is still not today. You will be throwing your entire life away if you marry him, probably throwing away your career as well."

"And what do you know about either one? You are unbelievable, mother. You know nothing of my life and even less about my career that I have built from nothing and with no help from you. I—no, we— defied the odds, mother, and we are together now despite all of your attempts to keep us apart. Yes, I know all of it! How could you do it, mother? Explain it to me, please."

"Why? You seem to have it all figured out, so why do you need me to say it?"

"You're wrong, mother. I have no answers to why you were hell bent on destroying my every happiness. First, it was daddy; you hated any attention he gave to me. Next, it was Seamus. I loved him so much, and I tried to talk to you about it, but you never seemed to care. You called me stupid, a foolish girl that does not know any better. You mocked me time and time again, and then you took him away from me. Your actions broke my heart and shattered it into a million pieces. You knew how broken I was when we returned home, and you never once tried to comfort me. I cried so many tears, the staff had to wash my bedding daily because my sheets were drenched with my tears. Even then, not one hug! Nothing from you. Why mother? Why?"

"He would have hurt you sooner than later if I did not stop it when I did. What did you know about love at fifteen? You were so starry-eyed it made my stomach turn over. You lost yourself over a boy who was older and should have known better than to show any attention to you."

"You make it sound as if he was twenty years older than me. He was eighteen, I was fifteen! My god, mother, we were kids! We should have been free to explore our feelings and just enjoy our time together being in love with the other. We didn't do anything wrong, mother. My love with Seamus was beautiful. It *is* beautiful, but you made it ugly and set out to destroy it."

"I did what had to be done, Shaena. I will not apologize to you or anyone, for that matter. As for your father, he didn't have time to play tea party or dress-up. His role was to provide for his family and make sure we were taken care of. You never had to worry or need anything because I was the driving force behind his work ethic. You should be thanking me instead of behaving like a sniveling, whiny, petulant child."

"Tell me about Colin."

"Excuse me?"

"You remember Colin, don't you, mother? The love of your life, the one that you wanted but in turn, did not want you. Can he be the reason why you hate love?"

"Get out of my home, and do not return."

"Try again, mother. I am not going anywhere until you tell me why."

"What do you want from me? Yes, I hate love and everything that love represents! I hate, and that is Colin O'Toole's fault. He broke my heart. He fooled me with his charms and made me believe we had a future together, but then he left me and I was alone. I would have done anything for him, anything, but he still did not want me. Imagine my surprise years later when our paths crossed again. The moment I saw your Seamus, it was as if I had Colin back. After I made the connection, I did go to him and practically threw myself down to his feet, but again he refused me. What would you have me do? I could not trust his son with my daughter and have you suffer the same fate."

"You threatened Colin, mother. You used me to get what you wanted, and when that failed, you made it your mission to destroy what I had with Seamus. After his parents discovered the truth behind our sudden exit from Kildare, his father told him the truth about your relationship. It hurt him so much to see how his son was suffering, never knowing what became of me. When hope returned, Seamus came to New York and found daddy, never giving up hope that we would reunite, and you intervened again. Daddy believed in love, and for whatever reason, he loved you."

"He was a fool, and clearly so are you."

"Okay, I'll be a fool. I will be the biggest fool in the world, because I have love in my life, in my heart, and deep in my soul. You are cold, malicious, and alone. I would have to care to feel sorry for you. I came here today believing that I would confront you with all I knew, and then you would feel bad and apologize."

"Sorry to disappoint you, but I'm not sorry. He and his father are cut from the same cloth, and Seamus will hurt you as Colin hurt me. When he does, Shaena, I will not lose any sleep over it, and the only thing I will offer you in return is a big fat 'I told you so.' But before that inevitable tragedy happens, please give your future father-in-law my regards."

"I'm afraid I cannot do that, mother."

"Why?"

"Colin O'Toole is dead, along with his wife. It was an accident that claimed their lives, but Seamus survived. Before Seamus and his family took that fateful trip, they wished for their son to find me, as we were meant to be. Years would go by before that happened, mother. While you were living your cold and—what you believe to be a— meaningful life, I was existing in mine. You see, mother, I thought I was happy. I was number one at my job. I had the great apartment. What I did not have was love. I was alone, and all the while, Seamus was fighting for his life on the other side of the world. You knew he came for me, mother. You could have had the power to prevent all of this tragedy for your daughter, but you said nothing."

"So, what will you have me do now? I have listened to you and all of your ranting. If you want to throw your life away and marry the 'love of your life,' then go right ahead. I will not stop you, but these doors are closed to you. You have made it clear where your loyalty lies, and it is not with me. So go, Shaena. Leave this house, and take your fiancé with you."

"You really are choosing to send me away, aren't you, mother? You will not admit any wrongdoing, and you will not apologize for anything?"

"Yes, yes to all of it."

"Okay, I tried. I don't know why I thought I could appeal to your human side, but you have made it clear to me that you do not possess one. Take care, Charlotte."

TWENTY-SIX

You Had Your Chance

Seamus

After the calls I made and an interesting conversation with Charles, I tried with my best effort not to eavesdrop, but when I heard Shaena crying, I knew I had to go to her.

"Oh, my sweetheart, please don't cry," I called out to her.

"You were right, Seamus. This was so wrong to come here. I should have listened to you."

"No, you shouldn't have. I had my reasons to hate her, but I never wanted that for you. She is your only living parent, and it was not my place to interfere with your relationship. I'm so sorry, baby."

"You're wrong, Seamus. You have every right to tell me anything, because I'm yours, and you're mine. Take me home."

She gave Charles a hug. This time, he knew it was goodbye. I asked Shaena to wait for me in the car. She looked at me hesitantly, but I gave her a reassuring look that I would be okay. She fought the good fight against her mother, and sadly, she lost. I promised myself that if we ever reunited, I would never allow anyone to hurt my girl again, not even her mother.

"You're still here? I would have thought you would be on your way to the airport by now. You look different from the boy I knew, who used to look like his father. Why is that?" Charlotte said to me.

"You are unreal. You never change."

"Not like you."

"Well, twenty-seven surgeries will have that effect on one's appearance. My face may be different, but I am still the same man that loves your daughter, maybe the only one that ever truly did. You are pure fucking evil, and do not even dare to breathe my father's name. He was a good man, one who loved me and my mother with all that he had. What you believe you had was just dreamt up in your mind from the delusions of a young and impressionable girl. Get over it, woman! You just allowed your greatest accomplishment to walk out of your door, and if I have anything to say about it, you will never lay eyes upon her again. You do not deserve her, you never did. You fuck with Shaena again, and I promise you that I will strip you bare of everything you own."

"Go to hell!" she screamed. "You can't do anything to me, and all I have to do is snap my fingers, and my daughter will come back, like she always does."

"Those days are over, Charlotte, and I can do more than you think. Take this apartment, for one. I own it, and all the possessions in it. You see, a couple of years ago, you mortgaged this home and your possessions to pay back...what do they call it here in America...'Uncle Sam?' Well, your loan was not met, and therefore all went into foreclosure. *I* paid your debt, and then some. So you, bitch...I own your miserable ass. Oh, and by the way, I own the rest of the building too."

"No! I don't believe it. You are lying. My lawyer handled everything for me."

"You mean Peter McGivney?"

"Yes, he's my lawyer. What do you know of it?"

"No, I'm afraid not. Peter McGivney works for me, along with my arsenal of lawyers I retain. You have only been able to remain in this lifestyle because it is one, which I have provided for you. I could not win back Shaena's heart and have her mother on the street while I did it, but now that is over. I have Shaena back, and clearly, you have kicked her to the curb, so why should I be generous at this point? Consider this your notice to vacate my building immediately. I am sure Charles will assist in packing your things. Oh, and don't worry about your trusted employee. He and I had a long discussion earlier. I will make sure he receives a generous severance package and happily retires in peace."

"No! You cannot do this to me. I have friends all over the world. They will help me, and then I will make you pay for what you have done. When Shaena finds out, she will never forgive you for hurting me."

I gripped her thin, bony chin and held her in place. She was vile, this I knew, but like Shaena, I held out hope for her.

"You listen to me, Charlotte Blake, because I never repeat myself twice. You will never hurt my love again. You will never even breathe her name. I will make it my life's mission to make her forget you once we drive away from here today. However, you, dear, will certainly think of me every single day of your miserable existence. You will remember today. You will remember every disgusting word you have said to your daughter, and each night those words will replay out in your dreams. Your hate will haunt you nightly, and you will lose yourself in darkness because you have no light in your heart. You just let the best thing walk out of your life. I will protect her, and give her happiness all the days of her life."

I released her with a shove, and for once, she might have looked remorseful, but it was too late. I turned and never looked back.

As I walked out of the building, my girl leaped from the limo with tears in her eyes. She ran right into the safety of my embrace. I picked her up, held her shaking body, and calmed her.

"I love you, sweet girl. I am so sorry you ever had to go through that. I love you. I love you."

"I love you, too. Please, Seamus, take me away. Take me home to Kildare."

I never wanted anything more than to bring Shaena back to Ireland. I knew she was hurting and not in a great place after her disastrous reunion with her mother. I would hold her throughout the night and reassure her how much she meant to me.

She was not broken, far from it. She was hurting over the loss of her mother, but some people were not redeemable, no matter how hard you tried to change them. We would take tonight to rest, see her boss, and then leave for home.

Goodbyes were always hard to do especially with the ones you love. After tomorrow, she would say goodbye to her painful past so that she could begin a new future with me.

TWENTY-SEVEN

When the Clouds Part, Let There Be Light

Shaena

"**A**re you ready, love?" Seamus asked me, as I remained seated in the limo.

My eyes peered through the window up at the tall skyscraper that housed Prestige Publishing, a place where I thought I ruled the world, where Monday was my favorite day because it was War Room day. But today would be different. Today I would begin a new chapter in my career and say goodbye to the team who became a family to me when my own turned their backs on me. Seamus sat quietly, rubbed his hand over my thigh and made me wish we never left my bed this morning.

"When we go in there, my boss, James, is going to be all over me. He's going to be celebrating as if God himself just handed him the golden ticket to the pearly gates. He lives and breathes this work, and gaining Weston James is the biggest notch on his victory belt."

"I can handle James Gentry. I have met many men like him in my life."

"He's a good man, Seamus. He's just driven like the rest of us."

"Look at me, Shaena," he said to me, his stare was hypnotizing and pulled me in.

"I never intended my work to become anything more than the road that led back to you. I don't know how many more times I can explain this to you. It has made me a great deal of money—money I never needed or even wanted. I made myself a promise that I would give James what he desired most, no matter what happened between us."

"Wait. I'm sorry, but I'm going to have to switch from fiancée to publishing agent. Is there a book or not, Seamus?" I asked.

TWENTY-EIGHT

More for Me to Write

Seamus

I had led Connor to believe that I had not written anything new, but that was a lie. A writer never stops writing. I knew when I penned *The Vanishing Raven* that the sequel could only have one ending I could live with: *The Raven Returns*, and she did. Could I trust her publishing house to release our love story out into the world? If Shaena trusted our story in their capable hands, then I guess I could too, but only under her watchful eye.

"Yes, there are many, but I am only interested in publishing one," I told her.

"Our book?"

"Yes, our book. *The Raven Returns* will be a bestseller, I promise. Then, I will put Weston James to rest and work in the only role I ever wanted. I want to be your husband. I want to be a father to our children. I want to love you, take care of you, and I want my kisses to erase all the hurt from your heart. When I see you smile, I want to know I was the one who made that happen. How does that sound to you love?"

Wiping away her tears, I cupped Shaena's face and kissed her.

"It sounds wonderful, something out of a romance novel, a story I would definitely want to read," she said.

"How about living it?"

"There's nothing I want more, but on one condition."

"Anything, baby, I will give you anything."

"Don't give up on your work. Your gift is too beautiful not to share with the world. For a long time, it was the only thing I had in my life, and it helped me breathe."

"I'm sorry I didn't come sooner for you. I love you, Shaena. No one will ever hurt you again, least of all your mother."

"I believe you, Seamus, but she's the last thing I'm thinking of. I just want you, so let's go upstairs and have a little fun with James."

TWENTY-NINE

Delivering the Contract

Shaena

"**W**elcome home, Shaena. You look lovely."

"Thank you, James, it was…um…a good trip," I said to my boss as I looked over to Seamus, who was waiting to be introduced.

"James, I would like you to meet my fiancé, Seamus O'Toole. Seamus, this is James Gentry, my boss and the owner of Prestige Publishing."

As I watched James and Seamus exchange pleasantries, I could not help to notice the wicked grin playing out all over Jesse's face. Clearly, something had changed between the two men while I was away. His just-fucked hair was his telltale. He was shameless with his flirting, devilish, and charming smile. He winked over at me, confirming what I believed to be true. Good for him! We all took a seat in the conference room, with James unbuttoning his jacket.

"You never cease to surprise me, Shaena. Here I send you to Ireland to gain our house a new client, and not only do you accomplish your job, but you meet, fall in love with, and are engaged to an Irish man. Well done, my friend, well done!"

"Not exactly in that order, James, but let's just table that story for another time. You are right about landing a new client. Weston James has agreed to sign with Prestige for a one-book deal."

"What?" James had barked at me before I could finish.

"If you would allow me to go on, I will explain."

"Fine!" he grumbled under his breath.

"Now, this is not how the game is played—we know this—but with securing an author like Weston James, we as his publishing house have to be amendable. A one-book deal is not what you or I were hoping for, but it is what we have now. When I was in Ireland with him, we discussed this in detail and his reasons behind it. Unfortunately, I have signed a non-disclosure agreement to that conversation, so James, you will just have to trust me. Our deal with Weston James will be conducted as a trial basis. He never locks in with any house until he sees what they can deliver, as stated here in this contract."

I handed it over to James with his eyes wide and blazing with anger.

"Are you fucking with me? He actually wrote up a contract for us? What happened to the one I sent with you?"

"Our contract became worthless the minute I pitched it to him. I believe there are some ashes of it still lingering in the fireplace where he burned it before my very eyes."

"This is outrageous. You should have called me immediately. I would have had you on the next plane back to New York."

"Now, what fun would that have been? Go on, James, read the contract."

James began flipping through the pages of the contract while my eyes shifted over to Seamus. He wasn't giving anything away. Seamus appeared to be enjoying this, and the exaggerated story I was telling James. He winked over at me, and I knew he was encouraging me to take the lead and have fun. Hell, I deserved this challenging banter after what I endured with my mother.

Normally Connor handled all of Weston James's negotiations, but this, he said, he would not miss for anything in the world. *The Raven Returns* was personal for him as *The Vanishing Raven* before it. It was our love story in black and white, and he needed to remain in complete control of it.

"Well, James, do we have a deal?" I asked.

"I would be a fool to say no, but Shaena, nothing changes? How can he expect to remain in the dark? All he wants from us is to publish his book. Any house can do that. I wanted more. I wanted to introduce him to the world as our client, the new face of Prestige. The only thing he has changed is the house itself. The deal is the same, and one that I'm not sure I want."

"James, I caution you that if you walk away from what Weston James is offering, I can almost guarantee this opportunity will not come around again for you. I've met this man. I can assure you he is the real deal, and his work speaks for itself. You want to know why he doesn't want to step out from the shadows. It's simple, James, because he can. Do you believe he is the first great mind to have some quirks? What about Hemingway? What about Salinger? Now we can chat for days on end about both of them, but I don't have that kind of time. You have a contract from Weston James. This is what you said you wanted. I have delivered it. The clock is ticking, James. Either you sign it and the real work begins, or I rescind it and call it a day."

"You rescind it? You're joking, right. Did your trip to Ireland make you forget who the fuck you work for?"

I remained silent as I looked over to Seamus, who was now up from his seat, ready to hand James his ass. I quickly stepped in between my beautiful man and pig headed boss. Jesse was being unusually quiet, looking back and forth to James and Seamus. Seamus's sapphire eyes have turned red, I knew he wanted to defend my honor, but he did not need to. I could handle James all on my own, and I silently prayed he knew it by looking into my eyes. He softened under my gaze, and then winked. My man was back.

"Jesse, can you please show Seamus around, and I should be along shortly," I said.

I raised myself up on my tiptoes to kiss Seamus and show him I was okay. After Jesse and Seamus left, I turned back to James.

"I don't want to hear it, Shaena. How the hell do you expect me to react to this bullshit contract?"

"I expect you to be goddamn grateful! Do you even know what you are holding in your hands? Weston James has written the sequel to *The Vanishing Raven*. Therefore, if the guy wants to keep his privacy, he would not be the first and certainly not the last to do so. Now, be smart about this, James, because you only have a small window of time left."

"Wow, you certainly have returned with some new, fired-up spirit, now haven't you?"

"Not really, I'm still the same agent that left here with one goal in mind: sign the client. You are the one that's acting all weird. In addition, I haven't forgotten who I work for, but I would advise you to watch your tone the next time you decide to have a hissy fit in front of my fiancé. He was one inch away from beating your ass. And yeah, he would have no hesitation if I had not stopped him. So can we talk?"

"What do you want me to say? I'm sorry, okay. I guess I'm all fucked up in my head right now, and the mystery of Weston James or whoever he is just drives me mad. You did good, you always do."

James then took out his gold pen and signed the marked pages of the contract I had presented him with.

He said to me, "Here you go, boss, he's all yours."

If only James knew how true, that statement was.

"So, James, now that I'm engaged to Seamus…"

James interrupted me. "Shaena, I know what you're going to say, and I want to stop you right there. You are my best agent. You've brought in this house's top clients. You don't have to give notice, and you don't have to quit just because you are getting married or moving.

I cannot afford to lose you. Please consider my offer before saying anything further."

"Wow, James. You don't know how much that means to me. Thank you! I will definitely let you know my answer once things are fully settled with me and Seamus."

Once the smoke cleared and James was calmer, I knew this would probably be my only opportunity to butt my nose into his business.

"What's going on here, James? You looked like the Cheshire cat when I walked in. Have things changed between you and Jesse?"

"Leave it alone, Shae, okay?"

"Fine, I will just ask Jesse."

As I made my way to the door, he called out for me.

"Yes, James," I asked.

"How do I keep him, Shae?"

The tone he used was raw and laced with something I had not heard before…fear.

"That's easy, James. You love him. You love Jesse with everything you have, and when you plant your feet firmly to the ground and face tough times, you stay. My best friend needs you to stay and fight for him and for what you have been denying for far too long now. You are the one, James, the one he wants. I think the bigger question remains: do you feel the same for him? I am telling you straight, if you do not own up to your feelings for Jesse finally, then you are going to lose him. Do you hear me, James? You will lose him. He wants a hell of a lot more than just random hook-ups or a quickie in the coat closet. He wants a commitment; he wants you."

"And I want him! Do you think I am just messing around? You know me better than that, Shaena, and he does too. I have done this before, and it scares the shit out of me. Sure, everyone knows I'm gay—I do not hide it—but I do not flaunt it either. For so long, all I have had is my work—this work—that you and I are pretty fucking great at."

"Sounds familiar, because I was the same way until Seamus

O'Toole put this ring on my finger."

"Damn! I can't believe you are engaged. Here I am, thinking I have it all figured out, and then Jesse entered my life so unexpectedly. I wasn't ready for him. He's in my heart, mind, and soul. How do I even rationalize that? My head is spinning out of control, and with every step we take forward, I am afraid I'm going to fuck it up and fall a foot backward."

"Doesn't it feel good?" I asked him.

"What?"

"To admit your true feelings. It must be a huge weight off your chest."

"Yeah, I guess it is, but how do I know Jesse won't change his mind six months down the road?"

"I guess you are going to have to stick around to find out."

"Okay, he wins...we win. He's worth taking a risk for, and if I'm going to leap, I want to hold Jesse's hand and know he will not let me fall."

We both turned to see Jesse standing in the doorway, with Seamus smiling off to the side. He then made quick strides and took James into his arms. Finally! The two men kissed and sealed their fate with one another. Love was the sledgehammer that broke down the protective walls that James concealed himself behind. No matter what Jesse told me, I knew he never gave up hope, and clearly, I was lucky enough to bear witness to it.

I grabbed hold of Seamus's hand, and we made a quiet exit from James's office, leaving the lovers to their bliss.

"I see you have the signed contract," Seamus said to me.

"Was there ever any doubt?"

"Not a chance, lass. My money was always on you."

We walked with our hands entwined to my office, where I would pack up my belongings, and then to my apartment to do the same. My heart was leading me home...home to Kildare. Seamus carried my boxes to the bay of elevators, and I began laughing with gusto. Seamus was dying to know what I was thinking of, and once we were in the privacy of the elevator, I told him.

"You picked Weston James as your alias, and now my best friend, Jesse, is in love with a man named, James. Do you see where I'm going with this? Jesse James? Oh my goodness! I love the coincidence of it all, and I wish I could tell Jesse, but I promise, my love, I will never tell. I'm just happy."

"I can see that, darling, and you better get used to it, because you will feel nothing else for the rest of your life."

THIRTY

Welcome Home

Shaena

After James signed the contract, Seamus was more at ease. He would have Connor take care of anything else needed. Working on a book was the last thing Seamus cared to do at the moment. He wanted out of New York as soon as possible. He helped me pack, and it was funny because all I left with was two boxes. My belongings in my apartment would not be that much more. The furniture and possessions I had were just material things, I had no emotional attachment to any of it. I had everything I needed the minute I reunited with Seamus. I could not wait to return to Ireland.

My mother had called and left messages for me to call her back. She sounded frantic on my voicemail. I didn't think I was ready for that, considering how we left things between us. She clearly was set in her ways, unwilling to change. Seamus left it up to me to decide to contact her, but I believe it pleased him to know I had no want to see nor speak with her.

Jesse had come over with take-out bags in one hand, wine in the other.

"We are so drinking tonight," he called out as he made his way into my kitchen.

Seamus smiled as he looked up from his laptop. He had warmed up to Jesse over the last few days and was genuinely happy for him and James.

"Will James be joining us?" I asked as I pulled down some plates from the cabinet.

"He sends his love and will call you next week once you are settled over in Kildare. Although I would love to be in any proximity of him, he knew this was *our* night. I'm going to meet up with him later at his place."

"So things are going well between you two?" I questioned.

"For now, yes. We are taking it slow, but we both agreed to try and see where it leads."

"I am so happy for you and him! Oh, I love it when I'm right."

"Yeah, me too. I would welcome a thousand 'I told you so's' to have the same outcome."

"You have it, Jesse. You and James are going to make it, and believe me, I know what I am talking about when it comes to matters of the heart. A long time ago, I left my heart in Kildare, where I lost my faith in love and did not believe I would ever feel it again."

"Your mother is some piece of work. I cannot believe she pulled all of that shit on you. She's been calling the office for you."

"I'm sure she has, and what have you told her?"

"The truth. You left the office and to stop calling, because I have no idea where to forward the messages to."

"Yeah, that will hold her off for a little while, but with Seamus stripping her of everything she has, I don't expect to see her in Ireland anytime soon."

"How do you feel about that? Your guy has balls for sweeping in and playing corporate raider."

"He did what he had to do, and I am not going to fault him for it.

Seamus had many reasons to even the score with my mother. I truly believe he would have been merciful if she had shown any compassion and willingness to make amends with me, but she did not. Anyway, I do not want to spend the rest of our night talking about Charlotte Blake. Did you bring any orange chicken?"

For the rest of the night, Jesse and I talked about my upcoming wedding. Of course, it would be held in Ireland, probably in my new castle. Seamus had given me a little more background to his family's wealth, which he was now the sole heir to and in control of.

I was still in a bit of a foggy haze about how much my life had changed in the few short weeks I had been reunited with Seamus. Although I physically left Prestige and New York, my employment status was intact. I would be directly working for Weston James, and that delighted me to no end. After all, the man behind the words owned me, body and soul, so I'm sure I could easily adjust to my new role as naughty agent.

Kidding aside, in the contract James had signed, Weston was very specific to whom he wanted to work with. I would serve as the liaison between him and Prestige. James no longer questioned his diva-like demands, and he let me handle it. At the end of the day, Prestige was front and center and was the house that would reap the benefits *The Raven Returns* would bring.

"I love you, best friend. What am I going do without you? This apartment holds so many memories for us. If these walls could talk, your guy Weston would have another hit on his hands."

"I have no doubt that Weston will come up with best sellers, but our story is between you and me, and I will always cherish our memories."

"Don't make me cry, you bitch. Damn! I love you, Shae, and your guy better freaking rock as a husband, or my threat still stands and I will kick his ass."

"I love you, too."

We hugged, and I placed my head on his shoulder and thanked

God I was lucky enough to have known this amazing man. Jesse then put his arm around my shoulder and called over to Seamus.

"Hey, Irishman!"

I covered my mouth from laughing aloud. Jesse was very blunt, earning him an "I beg your pardon" expression from Seamus, who walked over to us.

"Yes, you were saying?" Seamus said.

"Take care of my girl. She's one of the special ones, okay?"

"I believe I already promised you, but I have no problem saying it again. Shaena is the one person I value most in my life, and she will be cherished every single day for the rest of her life. My treatment of her will make queens and princesses all over the world jealous."

"Now, that's what I want to hear. Take care, man. You're one of the good ones too."

"It takes one to know one. We will see you for the wedding. You *and* James?"

"Absolutely, try to keep us away."

"I wouldn't dream of it," Seamus replied, "and who knows… Shaena and I may be soon attending another wedding other than our own."

"That's the plan! Now all I have to do is convince James of it without scaring him to high heaven."

"We're pulling for you both."

"Thanks, man."

The two most important men in my life were becoming friends before my eyes, and all was right in our lives. I could not have asked for anything more. Damn, I should take up crying as a profession! They even managed to get a quick bro hug in before Jesse turned back to me.

"Stop crying. You're going to dry out your tear ducts."

"I can't help it. I'm going to miss you so much, and who's going to help me pick out my outfits?"

"That's what Skype is for. I'll see you soon, and then you can show me Kildare, okay?"

"Okay. I love you…take care of you."

"Love you more…take care of you."

That night, I was having the most amazing dream when soft lips on my neck caused me to wake from my sleep. I had curled my body as close as I could to Seamus, as he stroked his fingers up and down my back until I was in a jet-lag coma.

New York was hard on many counts. I wished I could have avoided the climactic ending to what was left of my relationship with my mother. Seamus encouraged me to write my feelings down in a journal he had given me. He said journal writing helped him a great deal when we parted, when he was recovering from his accident, and then sadly, when he was mourning the loss of his parents. I'm sure it was easy for him to write. He could openly express his feelings, while I liked to shut down and make myself forget.

He told me that I had to stop blaming myself for not coming back to Ireland sooner. We were both young, and it was part of a past that we can now say is complete. We were together now, so I knew eventually I would let it go.

Maybe hearing my mother admit her duplicity drove the point home for me. What scared me the most was the fact that she wasn't sorry. I knew I could not obsess over why Charlotte Blake was the way she was. I had to move on from the past and her, and with Seamus's help, I knew I would be able to.

"Hello, my love," I said as I tilted my neck back for him to have more access. I loved his touch and completely felt loved by him.

"Did you sleep well?"

"With you holding me? How could I not?"

"I love you, lass, so very much. Now, look out the window, because we are…home."

I did exactly as he asked, and I covered my mouth with my hand. The castle had been decorated and completely lit up with sparkling white lights. Every window was covered with a lighted star. It was breathtaking, not one fixture wasn't covered in lights. Fresh snow lined the gorgeous property.

I could not tear my eyes from what I was seeing. We missed so much time that I wanted my do-over right now. To make snow angels in the snow, to having a snowball fight and having Seamus chase me until he caught me in his strong arms. Yes, this was what I wanted. I was wearing his ring and I knew we soon would be married, but I wanted the dating part too.

Our car stopped, and Connor and Aideen greeted us. She was holding a bouquet of purple roses for me, and my heart screamed, "I love this man!" Seamus never missed an opportunity to show me how much he loved me.

As if he knew what I was thinking and feeling, he wrapped his arms around me and whispered in my ear, "Welcome back to Kildare, Shaena."

THIRTY-ONE

New Life

Shaena

We stepped inside, and the entryway as well as the rest of the castle was transformed into Christmas, which was only a week or so away. I knew we would not be living here for much longer. Seamus had another home not too far from here, which I've yet to see, but he promised we would go first thing in the morning.

I knew our time here was limited, with the castle reaching capacity for holiday visitors. Aideen had her hands full with arriving guests and all of the holiday accommodations, and now Seamus added our wedding to the list. He was an impossible man with determined ways of getting what he wanted. All he would have to do was flash his perfect smile to Aideen, and she would grant his every wish. She was so kind, and although I never met his mom, I could see how she has stepped into the role of caring for Seamus as a mother naturally would. Before my tears could fall, I shrugged off the negative thoughts that were about to creep in about my own mother. Aideen must have sensed my change in the air and brought me in for a hug.

"I think it's time for a spot of tea, wouldn't you agree?" she said comfortingly.

I shook my head in agreement, and the tears fell. She shooed Seamus off, and he took the hint. We sat in the atrium, with a fire blazing to warm the room.

"Please, Shaena, no more tears. Haven't you cried enough to last a lifetime?"

Her words held so much truth behind them.

"You're probably right, but I can't help myself. My mother would say that I was irrational, and her advice would be to tell me to suck it up and grow a spine."

"She's wrong, so wrong. I may not be able to fully understand what you went through when she forced you apart from Seamus, but I understand him and what it's like to be a parent. Forgive me for talking out of turn, but I have to say with my whole heart how much I believe you were just dealt a bad hand when it comes to parents. Mental abuse can be just as damaging as physical abuse. It breaks my heart that you had to endure that kind of pain in your life. I am so sorry, but she should be flogged for all of the tongue-lashings she spat at you over the years."

"You're right, she should, but I believe after the one she endured from Seamus, I think she may have gotten the point."

"Ah yes, he was always very protective, especially when it comes to how he loves. My dear friend, you must know how much he would move the world if only to give you another day of happiness. My opinions about your mother are my own, and I am sorry if I hurt your feelings by blatantly expressing them, but I can't bear to see you hurting over something you may never be able to change."

"I'm okay, Aideen, and thank you for sticking up for me. I guess it was time someone did. This is all I know, and if Seamus will be patient with me, I will do better, I promise."

"Did I hear my name?"

I squeezed my eyes closed in fear he may have heard what I just said. I took a breath and then turned to see my beautiful man.

"You did, because you were eavesdropping," I said to him.

"I wouldn't dare, my love. I was simply walking by on my way to my office."

"Okay, handsome, and you say that *I* don't lie well."

"Okay, I may have heard a word or two, but not anywhere near a conversation's worth. Forgive me, love?"

He placed a kiss on top of my head and left me with Aideen, who had not stopped smiling.

"What?" I asked her.

"You see? I told you."

"So you did, my friend."

"I must be getting back to work. We have a family of twelve arriving early in the morning, and I have to make sure all of their rooms are ready."

"Wow, you work so hard."

"Choose a job you love, and you will never have to work a day in your life."

"Confucius, right?"

"Right, and of course, Seamus's mother, Mary, used to say it to him all the time. She knew two things about her son: one, his love for you, and second, his passion for writing. Now my dear friend, he has both. Go rejoice in that, and be happy."

"I will, Aideen, on one condition."

"Name it."

"You take your own advice and do the same."

"Oh, my sweet girl, I already have."

She quickly hugged me and practically skipped out from the atrium. I guess love was not only in the air for me and Seamus, and Jesse and James, but for Aideen and Connor too!

I gently knocked on Seamus's study door to find him looking studious behind his desk. I rather liked this look to him. He was wearing his Armani black framed eyeglasses. He must have taken out his contacts when we returned home.

Home? I smiled on how much I loved saying, thinking, and feeling that word. I had never felt like I had a comfortable, warm, loving place before, and now I found it for the first time in my life with Seamus.

The great novels were written for couples like us. In just a few short weeks, he had shown me who we were. What we could be. What we would have for our future. He reignited my belief in what we lost all those years ago when we parted. Even when he revealed his identity, I still had doubts, but now, I could say they were forever gone. I would never question his love for me, my love for him, and—for lack of a better word—destiny. He was always meant to be mine. He told me that repeatedly in all of the times we were together. I loved him so much and could not wait to be his wife.

"How long are you going to stand in my doorway before I rush over and take you against the wall and have my way with you?" he called out.

"Just admiring the view, my love. How can I not, when I am looking at the most gorgeous author I have ever known?"

"This writer loves you and wants you to come over here…right now."

I could not resist him if I tried. His gaze alone had a drugging effect on me. I was hooked and so high on Seamus. I practically knocked him over when he took me in his arms. I never wanted to leave him, and I swear as I breathe, would never do so again.

"By the way, these sexy glasses of yours are turning me on, big time."

"Good to know. I will have to remember that."

He crushed his lips onto mine, and I moaned from his lustful kiss.

"I missed you just now," he said. "Are you okay, love? Did your talk with Aideen help?"

"It did, a great deal, as a matter of fact. She seems to pick up on my change of moods before I know it myself."

"She's a wonderful person, and with you coming back into my

life, I finally see how good she has been for me, and now for Connor. He is one stubborn man, but has seen the light when it comes to admitting his feelings for Aideen."

"I'm happy for them, and if he doesn't treat her well, I will show him some serious New York attitude."

"I do not doubt that for a minute, lassie, but rest assured, they're fine. They have been friends for a while and are taking it slow. It took a long time for Aideen to recover from her broken marriage."

"I guess everything happens for a reason."

"That's exactly what I have been trying to convince you of. Clean slate all around and it begins today!"

"I thought it already had."

I kissed Seamus again, and began nuzzling his neck.

"You are making me forget my own name when you touch me like that. Let me finish what I was going to say, and then I will let you have me anyway you please," he said.

"Oh really? In that case, continue and hurry, please."

Seamus moved me off his growing erection, and I sat on his desk to face him. His cheeks turned three shades of red. I loved how my touch turned him on, but I calmed myself so he could talk.

"As I was saying: clean slate. I've had some time to think about how I wrote *The Vanishing Raven* and how I will complete *The Raven Returns*. As I have already explained to you my reasons for writing the first book, I have to admit that I was not in a great place back then. I think back to when I was with your father and how hopeful he looked when he learned of my plans to find you. When he died, I have to admit a part of me was scared that the dream of finding you was lost too."

"I'm sorry, Seamus. I am ashamed to be her daughter. If she hadn't interfered, our lives could have been so different, and maybe not only your parents, but my father may still be alive today."

"Oh, love, I'm the one that should be regretful. I didn't mean to bring up sad memories for either one of us. I know what the first book represented, but as I have explained, my mind and heart was not in a great place. Overwhelmed by my struggling emotions, I felt as if I was losing you all over again and making you unattainable for me to reach. That book was layered in darkness because of my anger toward Charlotte. I promised you the next one would be everything it needs to be and so much more. You are every writer's inspiration by just breathing. You are so beautiful, and I do not mean just on the outside."

He placed his hand over my heart, and I nearly lost my breath.

"Your beauty is here. Your smile rights every wrong in my life. Your touch erases all my pain and loss. Your love sets me free and gives me hope to believe in us. We are going to have an amazing life together, and from this moment on, the past does not matter anymore. It shaped us, but it does not define who we are. No one knows us better than we do ourselves. I need this new start with you. Please, my love, will you be able to give me what I need?"

We lost so much. I would never allow Seamus to lose anything else. I would do anything for him. I would say yes to any request, and if he needed me to leave the past where it belonged, then I would give it to him. To look into the eyes of the only man I had ever loved made my decision easy. He would never push me, maybe nudge a bit, but ultimately he knew it would have to be me to find the closure on my own.

"Yes, I can."

"Really? You do not have to agree because you believe it's what I want to hear. I need it, Shaena, but not at your personal expense."

"I know, and you should know I would not do anything I was not comfortable with. As far as I am concerned, my mother made the decision she could live with, and I have as well."

"Shaena, I would not want you to regret your decision or resent me in the long run. You lost your father, but you still have a living parent, I cannot expect you to just behave like she does not exist."

"No, you're wrong. She stopped being a mother to me a long time ago, maybe even before she decided to annihilate us with her hate and jealousy. She had one last chance that I afforded her, and she did not relent. What does that tell you about her? She is a vicious person with no conscience nor unwillingness to change. I am done. It took my heart breaking all over again with learning the truth, and your love putting me back together again to see who she is. Our life has no room for someone like that. Family lives in your life. They know the smallest details about you and care about you regardless. We may not have our parents, but we are not alone either. You had Connor and Aideen. I had Jesse. We are not alone, my love. If anything, our life is fuller than ever."

"How did I get so lucky?"

"Ha! You are asking *me*, Seamus? I am the lucky one and am so in love with you. Now, my sexy Irish man with perfect freckles, take me to bed, make me forever yours, and then tomorrow we will plan the rest of our life."

"Beginning with our wedding?"

"Exactly…our wedding."

Seamus carried me off to our bedroom and told the staff not to disturb us. I was thankful this part of the castle was private and ours to use. He smiled wickedly at me.

"Feel free to scream as loud as you want…my quarters are soundproofed."

THIRTY-TWO

A Christmas Surprise

Seamus

Shaena's reaction to my estate overlooking Wicklow Mountain was as I had expected. She leaped into my arms and could not tear her eyes away from the spectacular view. I knew I could never live in my family's home after they died. The memories were too hard to bear without my parents to share them with. Buying this estate was just another step in wiping the slate clean and beginning over, and now I got to share this home with the love of my life.

"You never slept here, not even once?" she asked with wide eyes.

"Not one day," I winked back at her.

"Why ever not? This home is a dream. I cannot imagine what it would be like waking up to this view every morning and not be compelled to write. You must be so inspired."

"Why, thank you, my love. And you're right about inspiration. It was you, after all, that got me here, and now we will wake up every morning looking at the same incredible view together. This is where

I'm going to marry you. Right here in front of this view."

"Seamus, I…"

"What is it? Talk to me. No matter what it is, I'll fix it for you."

Shaena's beautiful porcelain skin was turning ashen, and she was beginning to scare me. Was she having second thoughts? She turned back to the view and gripped the railing of the second floor deck off our master bedroom suite. She exhaled and turned to reach for my hands. Once we touched and linked our hands together, she calmed.

"I can't help you love if you don't tell me what's wrong," I assured her.

"Oh, Seamus, everything is right. How did I get here when a month ago I was so lost? In a short time, you have changed my life. You can probably have anyone in the world to choose as your wife, and yet, you chose me. Forgive me, I'm just trying to catch up here. I'm in a complete haze of you, and it's out-of-this-world amazing."

I didn't need to hear one more word from her. She had been torn open with bleeding wounds for far too long now, and it was time to heal and move on together. I held her close. I kissed her gently and carried her back to our bed, where we made love. I was determined to erase the mark her mother left on her, and show her every day how much I adored and cherished her.

While Shaena slept and recovered from the rigorous workout we just had, I took time to finalize all of the arrangements for her surprise. I knew she would love the home I had purchased with only her in mind. I had the entire estate renovated to a more modern look with all of the amenities to keep us comfortable, but also maintaining the rustic feel of living up in the mountains.

The Barberstown Castle offered a reprieve to me when I need to get away and regroup, but with Shaena back in my life, I would no longer use that home as a place to hide. All I wished to do was live out in the open with Shaena and let light into my life.

Connor called me, and it was through a video chat joined with Aideen as well.

"Hello, sir, is Shaena with you?" Aideen asked.

"She's sleeping, and we have to make this quick before she wakes."

"Understood. Mr. Dempsey has received his itinerary, and his guest will be Mr. Gentry. They will arrive the day after tomorrow and shall stay here until the wedding. At that point, they will join you at your home. Miss O'Donnelly and her staff will begin prepping your home and property on Christmas Eve morning. The dressmaker has delivered Shaena's gown, and I must say it is breathtaking like the woman who will be wearing it. I will personally deliver the dress to Shaena myself, once you give me the okay. Sir, everything is under control. You are going to give Shaena a magical day."

"It sounds perfect. Thank you so much, Aideen, for all of your hard work."

"It's my pleasure, sir."

"Connor, what about the matter we discussed?"

"It's all been taken care of, sir."

"Excellent. Thank you for handling that personally for me."

"As Aideen said, it's my pleasure, sir."

I heard a creak at the door. Shaena was awake and about to walk in.

"Okay, that's all for now. I will call you back once the other matter is finalized," I whispered to the two of them.

My chat ended just as she made her way in through my office and to me.

"Come here," I summoned her to her usual spot, where I could hold her.

"Thank you for taking care of me. Sorry I fell asleep on you."

"Darling, I believe we took care of each other, and you needed the rest."

"Why is it that men always have sex on their minds? I wasn't exactly referring to that when I said thank you."

"Is it my fault that I am in love with a gorgeous and insatiable woman who I can't keep my hands off of?"

"Okay, when you put it that way."

Oh, my love was smiling again, and it was the perfect time to reveal all my plans.

"Are you up for talking? I have something I would like to share with you, and I'm hoping it will make you happy."

"Oh Seamus, everything you do makes me happy. I don't believe there is anything you can do to top this elation!"

"Wrong, my love, but thank you. I will never stop making you happy. You are my dream come true. After your reaction to the house, and my bold statement about marrying you here, I wasn't sure if I had overstepped. I don't ever want to pressure you into anything you are not ready for. You have to be honest with me and talk it out. It's the only way I am going to know what's going on inside that head of yours."

"I'm sorry, Seamus. The last thing I want to do is hurt your feelings. I love the house. I love that we will marry here someday. It is perfect, all of it."

"That's wonderful. Here, my love. Come, let me show you something."

I stood up, still holding Shaena in my arms, and carried her to the stair landing. Kissing her lips, I left her there, walked downstairs, and turned to look up at her.

"What are you doing, you crazy man?"

"Loving you and making all of your dreams come true. I do hope you are ready for someday, because this Saturday on Christmas Day, I'm going to be standing right here and watching you walk down to me. You will be a vision in white."

"We're getting married on Christmas Day?" she asked, not quite believing what I just announced.

"Yes, we are. Are you ready to be my wife?"

"Yes!"

She began walking fast down the stairs. I quickly met her halfway and took her in my arms.

"I love you, Seamus. I can't wait to marry you."

"I love you, too. So much! We're getting married!"

I kissed her.

"Yes, we are," she said.

After we made love again and finally showered and ate lunch, it was time to have her dress delivered. The minute Shaena arrived at Barberstown, I had Aideen take care of her luggage. It was the only way to figure out her sizes, and once Aideen was sure, she contacted the dressmaker to begin designing her gown.

I felt bad about giving her a half-truth about Jesse. It was his idea to surprise her, and after he convinced me that she would love it in the end, I reluctantly agreed. He only talked to her briefly since we arrived, mostly about work and a little about James. After we said our goodbyes in New York, Jesse and James met at his apartment to talk. After they admitted their feelings to each other so openly at Prestige, their conversation continued in private. James asked Jesse to move in with him and give their relationship a chance. He had given Jesse the commitment he was hoping to have with him. Jesse didn't want to share his good news with his best friend over the phone. He needed to say it in person. He would also be the one to walk her down the aisle to me, another surprise I hoped would make her happy. Her father is gone, but there would be no one better suited to take his place than her best friend would.

She was curled up in front of the fireplace and reading a magazine when I walked in to join her.

"I have to say you look remarkably calm for a woman getting married in four days."

"I am, honestly, probably for the first time in a long while."

"Aren't you just the bit curious about our plans, or your dress for that matter?"

"Nope, not at all."

"Seriously?"

"As a three-book deal."

She winked and went back to her reading. This was the Shaena I knew and loved. When we met, she was shy and unsure of herself. As our relationship grew into something more, she began to trust her heart, and me. Shaena was bolder and blossomed under my affection and love that I had shown her.

"Always working," I said to her.

"Not today, my love. The only thing on my mind is my husband to be. You want to know why I can sit here so casually as if I don't have a care in the world?"

"The thought had crossed my mind."

"Easy, because I'm happy. You are making all my dreams come true. In a matter of forty-eight hours, your home has become my home. You announce we are getting married in four days from now, so this leads me to believe that you have everything under control. I am not worried about a thing, because I know my amazing Irish man with the freckles I love so much has taken care of every detail, and that includes my dress. Am I close?"

"You are perfect and correct on every point you just made. Thank you, lassie, for coming back to me."

"Thank you for sending for me."

I placed my forehead to hers and thanked God for this moment shared with her. The sound of the doorbell pulled me from my thoughts.

"Expecting anyone?" she asked.

"That would be Aideen with your dress."

"I knew it!" shouted Shaena, as she quickly kissed me and ran for the door. I watched the two women embrace, laugh, and leave, carrying her dress bag up the stairs.

"Thank you, Seamus! I love you." she called out to me.

"I love you, too, darling. Have fun."

"Hey, you have room for one more?" Connor said as he entered our home.

"By all means, come in. Let's go to my office where it's more private. So? Everything still okay?" I asked.

"Yes, it is. Her passport has been revoked, and she has no means to travel anywhere outside of the United States."

"Good, let's keep it that way. After all that she has put my girl through, Charlotte Blake has the audacity to attempt to get to her again. What is that leech thinking? I will never allow her to get in reach of Shaena again."

"As I stated, no worries, my friend. Charlotte Blake will remain where she is and will not do anything to interfere with your wedding."

"Connor, it's not just the wedding. I need her to be gone, and…forever. She is toxic to Shaena and to me. Shaena does not wish to have anything to do with her, especially after New York."

"I will monitor it from my side. You just concentrate on getting married."

"And your source at the Department of State? Are we all covered there?"

"We are."

"Thank you, Connor. What would I do without you and Aideen? You two have made all of this possible."

"My pleasure. I'll just add it to your invoice."

My friend and I shared a good laugh at that.

THIRTY-THREE

I Promise You

Shaena

Last night, we celebrated our first Christmas Eve together. It was magical. Seamus took us on a horse and carriage ride on the grounds of the Barberstown Castle. The snow fell on us as we stayed warm under a blanket and drank hot chocolate.

After all the needs of the castle's guests were met, it was our time to celebrate in private with our friends. Aideen had prepared a formal meal. It consisted of roasted duck, smoked ham, and a delicious array of vegetables, stuffing, and gravy. We finished with Christmas pudding and Earl Grey tea. It was perfect. I had never celebrated a holiday like this ever in my life, and all I could do was give thanks to God for this incredible blessing I had been given.

Before kissing me good night and retreating to a guest bedroom for the night, Seamus gave me one more gift, a tennis bracelet made up of sparkling emeralds that matched my engagement ring. On the clasp, a purple amethyst in the shape of a rose dangled from it. It was exquisite and custom-designed for me. Seamus kissed me passionately and lovingly as he recited a passage from the Corinthians, the Love is patient poem. He knew it by memory, of course he did.

Before I went to bed, I noticed that Seamus left a rose on my pillow with a note pinned to a ribbon tied around it.

Dear Lassie,

To the beautiful girl who crashed in to me when she did not believe anyone was watching…oh, how wrong she was! I was looking and wanted to know her. I knew I would fall hard the minute she stumbled in my arms. I caught her freely and wanted nothing more than to hold her and never let her go…my maiden with a silky mane of raven-colored hair that hung over her delicate shoulders as if it was a veil protecting her.

I love you with all of my heart and soul. Time has no measure on our love, and even when we were tested, we prevailed. And here we are, about to be husband and wife.

You, Shaena Blake, have my heart, always and forever. Tomorrow, in front of God and our witnesses, I will give you my heart and place it in your hands, freely, and promise to always cherish yours.

I hope you are ready, my love, because tomorrow is our wedding day, and it is time to get our happily ever after.

I will be waiting for you at the altar.

Love,

Seamus

It was the first time we slept apart, and I didn't like it. I slept on his side of the bed to be as close as I could. I swore that even if we ever fought, Seamus would have to still sleep in the same bed with me.

After waking up, I looked at my ring and matching bracelet on the same hand. The morning was such a whirlwind that I could barely catch my breath until I was already primped and dressed.

"You look absolutely beautiful."

"Thank you, Aideen," I said as I wiped a tear away. "You have been a great friend to me, and to Seamus. In a short time, you have filled a hole in my heart and replaced it with love and kindness."

"It is my honor to know you and love you. Now, let's get you married."

"I need a minute, okay."

"Take all the time you need, I'll be right outside."

I was thankful for the time to catch my breath. In a few minutes, I would be walking down the staircase to marry Seamus. This was once a dream, now a reality.

I was at the happiest point in my life, but at the same time, I felt a little sad. I missed my father. I wished he were here to give me away and do all the traditional duties a father was supposed to do at his daughter's wedding. I recited a prayer and hoped my father was looking over me today.

I took one more look at my appearance in the floor length mirror. Seamus had used the same vintage lace from his mother's wedding dress and had it transformed into mine. My back was open and framed with roses. The front was cut low into an empire waist, and again with a design of roses, lace, and crystals. He thought of everything, right down to the very last detail. My hair was styled into an elegant chignon, and I wore a tiara of diamonds with a matching veil attached to the back. All I needed now was my prince.

A knock to my door startled me, Aideen probably was worried that I would be a runaway bride, but there was no chance of that happening. I had loved Seamus since I was fifteen years old. This was our time, and I was beyond ready to become his wife. The knock became louder as I reached for the door.

"I'm coming," I called out.

I opened the door to see my best friend holding out his hand.

"It's about time, sunshine. Let's get you married."

"Jesse! What are you doing here?" I asked before rushing into his arms to hug him.

"Easy there, beautiful girl. If you wrinkle your dress before your big debut, that feisty woman out there will kick my ass."

"Aideen?"

"Yes, that's the one. She's great, but a little scary when you mess with her schedule. She's white knuckling her clipboard, so we need to go."

"I love you so much. You have never let me down, not ever. Thank you so much for being here today."

"I'll always be here for you, Shae. Best friends for life, right?"

"Always," I replied.

He handed me a tissue and said, "Dry those tears, and smile. You have waited a lifetime for this day."

"You're right, I have. I want to marry Seamus, and I cannot wait one more minute. By the way, what do you think of the dress?"

"Your guy did good. I approve."

Jesse held my hands, brought them up to his lips, and placed a gentle kiss on top of them.

He said, "You are absolutely stunning. I have never seen you look more beautiful in all the time I have known you. Before they send in a search party, I really have to get you down there. Shall we?"

I entwined my arm with his, and we made our way down the staircase to see Seamus waiting for me. He looked as if he belonged on the cover of a fashion magazine. He was wearing a custom-made, slim fit, two-button, navy blue business groom tuxedo. I had seen this same suit worn by Ryan Gosling for a red carpet event, and I had to have one made for Seamus. He would look fabulous in anything, but this suit really matched his eyes. I knew this was the one. Jesse laughed when I googled the picture. His response was: "Really, navy blue?" I quickly reminded him that the correct color would be sapphire, like my guy's beautiful eyes.

I was now in front of the man who I loved for nearly half my life, and I was home. Thank you God for bringing this beautiful man back to me.

"You're late," he whispered as my hand was now holding his. "No, my love, I'm right on time."

THIRTY-FOUR

The Day She Became Mine

Seamus

My heart nearly stopped when I saw my living angel walk up to where I was waiting. I knew she was thinking about how we got here, but it was really quite simple. Destiny brought us here because we were two bodies destined to become one. Shaena Blake was mine in every sense of the word, and no matter how high the decks were stacked against us, we defied them all.

Jesse had her hand in his, and after kissing it, placed it in mine. She smiled proudly at her friend, and then her eyes locked on mine.

We married in the company of those closest to us. Connor and Aideen were on my left. Jesse and James were on her right, and God was all around us.

We said traditional vows and then something personal.

"I love you, Shaena, that's no secret. You have been the compass that has guided me from the minute you crashed into me. You found me when I didn't know I was lost, and then when I actually was and drowning in so much pain that I knew what to do with, I was saved. I remembered the advice my parents gave to me, and I followed my heart. That heart has led me here, standing in front of you and promising you all that I have is now yours. It always was, my love."

My beautiful girl's eyes were sparkling brightly at me with a few tears threatening to fall. I knew they were happy ones. She handed her flowers to Jesse, and he handed her another tissue. She patted her eyes and then looked up into mine.

"It's my job to recognize talent, and when I read the words of someone brilliant, I felt so lucky to be able to do what I love. Little did I know that when I was invited to Kildare, I would find the love I left behind when I was fifteen years old, a love I believed was not made up from a young girl's imagination. I'm sorry I wasn't strong enough back then to fight harder for us, but I will now with all that I have. I want to be your compass as you serve as mine."

I was the one now crying, and it was Shaena tending to me. We whispered, "love you" to each other and then turned to face Father O'Byrne, who had known me since I was a boy. I could think of no other to marry us today.

He smiled, looked over to Shaena, and said, "I wish I had the privilege of knowing you when you were the young lass who fell in love with this scrappy one. Trust me when I say he has grown into a fine man. His parents and your father are shining over you and smiling from heaven. The beautiful vows you have taken here today of pledged devotion mean far more than you will ever know. May you always put those vows above anything that makes life smaller. I, for one, cannot wait to see what happens next."

He continued, "You've said your vows, you've exchanged your rings, so now we get to the best part. Seamus, Shaena, please join hands. You have come here today in front of your friends to bear witness to your union, and now you are a family. I now pronounce you husband and wife. You may kiss your beautiful bride."

With a roar of applause, I took Shaena and crushed my lips down to her beautiful mouth. No need to ask for entrance, she let me in mind, body, and soul. She was my soulmate, now and forever.

The celebration began as we danced our first dance as husband and wife. She never stopped smiling in-between her happy tears that fell.

"Thank you, Seamus, for making all of my dreams come true. Today was perfect. I will always cherish and remember it for the rest of my life. I love you, husband."

"I love you, wife, so very much. You will never know another day of sadness for as long as I draw breath, I promise you."

"I believe you, my love. If there is one thing I can count on is your promise. You knew all along we would have this day, didn't you?"

"Yes, I did. Love gives you hope and strength to overcome anything. Our story is living proof of that. Now, as much as I would love to keep dancing with you, you have an anxious best friend waiting his turn."

On her tiptoes, she kissed me and then turned to Jesse. He bowed down and extended his hand. They danced off to the side, where I expected he wanted some privacy to share his good news with her. I waited for a minute, and then she squealed as he twirled her around. They hugged and then continued dancing. Shaena was a believer, and all she wanted was for those around her to be happy. Her best friend now had the chance to do so. I left them to dance.

"Congratulations, sir."

"Thank you, Connor. Thank you for everything."

"No, *I* should thank *you*. If it wasn't for you pursuing your girl, I may have not found mine. I told Aideen that I loved her, and she in turn told me the same. For years, I thought I was content just living my life on my own, and after seeing how happy you were with Shaena, I realized the feelings I held back for Aideen was from fear of rejection. She had been put through the paces with that ex of hers, and if I so boldly put myself out there for her and then she turned me down, I thought I would have been crushed."

I replied, "Life is a risk and so is love. I can see how happy you have made Aideen. She deserves it all, Connor, and I know you are the right man for her, as she is perfect for you. Now, if you will excuse me, I have a wife to get back to."

"May I have this dance?" I asked as I approached the laughing trio of Shaena, Jesse, and James.

"Yes, you may, husband."

I picked her up effortlessly in my arms and carried her upstairs.

"What are you doing? We can't just leave the party, can we?"

"*Our* party, and yes we can. They will celebrate for hours, and the staff has everything under control. I want to make love to my wife, hold, kiss, and tell her how much I love her. Right now. How does that sound to you?"

"It sounds wonderful. Lead the way, my love."

THIRTY-FIVE

Epilogue

Shaena

L ife after our wedding was one blissful moment after another. Seamus and I remained in our bubble for nearly a month after the ceremony. Our new life was waiting for us outside of the protective walls of our country home. I loved it here. Seamus had built a beautiful home for us to share our lives in.

He had been hinting at trying for a baby on the night of our wedding, and I smiled and told him there was nothing I wanted more. We certainly had fun trying!

As for work, I was still handling the book release for *The Raven Returns*. James was anxious to set the publishing date. Seamus knew the direction he wanted to take with the book, and once he was sure of it, he wrote every day and night until he penned the last two words… The End.

It was beyond amazing, and what's more is that it is our true love story, a testament to our new life together. If Seamus were ever to change his mind about revealing his identity, then the world would know what I know. The world would read the truth behind the words and know the man who penned them, as well as the Raven who inspired him.

I only had to fly back to New York once since leaving with Seamus. I finalized the sale of my apartment, and then I spent a few days at Prestige finalizing the launch of the new book. Pre-sales were high, as much as the anticipation from the fans. I had convinced Seamus to create a website. He was completely against it at first, but after some major convincing on my part, he reluctantly agreed. We had linked the site with Prestige, so fans could keep up to date with the release and all of his projects. He wasn't ready to commit to anything beyond *The Raven Returns* at the moment, which James understood, but he hoped his house would have more projects by Weston James.

While I was in New York, I attempted to reconcile once again with my mother after learning she reached out to me before the wedding. I understood why Seamus needed to protect me, but I was not the scared fifteen-year-old anymore. I was a grown woman who made her own decisions. Sadly, I was good at fighting my battles with Charlotte Blake.

Charles had met me for lunch and simply handed me a letter. He looked crestfallen after delivering it to me. I assured him not to be, and I would be fine. As I placed the unopened letter in my bag, Charles brought me up to speed. She was now living quietly and under the radar in a small town upstate. When she left the city, she left the lifestyle behind as well. The lights had dimmed, and Page Six was no longer interested in the happenings of a former socialite's life. He was still on with her, and I was happy for that. To know she wasn't completely alone gave me comfort. Seamus told me repeatedly that I did not owe her anything, but she was still my mother, and I would never be so cruel to hurt her.

With all my professional commitments out of the way, I was ready for a night of junk food and old movies with Jesse and James. So far, they were managing living and working together, keeping the two separate. My best friend looked happy, and so did James. These were the moments I had always wished for them, and now they had it.

I called Seamus once I got settled on the plane that would take me home to him. He was in a foul mood and missed me terribly. I promised all sorts of naughty things I would do to him once we were alone. He laughed and told me he was holding me to it. No worries there, I was looking forward to it.

After the plane took off, I remembered my mother's letter was burning a hole in my purse, and I was fighting against my willpower to read it. It was only a few paragraphs.

Dear Shaena,

Please stop trying to reach out to me. I will turn you away each time, not because you did anything wrong, but because you did something right. You followed your heart despite of the many times I tried to stop you, and for once in your life, you are truly happy.

I never want to cause one more day of pain and tears I know will fall. I destroyed you, and I never said I was sorry. I'm saying it now, and although I do not deserve your forgiveness, I know you are a person with kindness and will unselfishly give it to me if I asked for it. I needed to say it. In truth, that is all the comfort I will get, knowing that I finally did.

If I may ask of one thing from you: please continue to live your life to the fullest with Seamus and the family you will have someday. You are no fool, my daughter, you never were. Jealousy and hate blinded me for years, and I never knew what I had until you were gone. It took losing everything to realize that. I am deeply sorry. I will spend the rest of my days hoping for absolution for my sins.

Yours,

Charlotte Blake

No tears fell after I finished reading it, only a sense of finality washed over me. Once again, my mother made a choice that she would have to live with, and I would do the same. I was okay, and I simply folded the letter and tucked it away into my bag. I had my closure a long time ago, and not even a letter could change that. All I wanted to do was be in the arms of the man I loved.

Two months later, *The Raven Returns* hit *The New York Times* and all international bestselling lists, surpassing book one's sales records. I was incredibly proud of Seamus. It never ceased to surprise me how fame did not affect him. All he cared about was for his words to bring meaning to someone's life, and they did to many.

On a warm day in May, we took a day trip to our gardens. It was the place Seamus first told me he loved me, and I could think of no other place to share my news with him. First, I wanted to give him a copy of *The Raven Returns*. The hardcover novel, beautifully embossed in gold lettering, was now in my hands. He had written our story, as promised. His dedication was another quote from John Keats, it read:

"Now a soft kiss—Aye, by that kiss, I vow an endless bliss."

How romantic and so like Seamus. The great poet was right on so many things, especially matters of the heart.

"Seamus, I have something for you," I said as I sat up to reach for my bag.

He was leaning up on his elbows, not a clue as to what my gift would be.

I said, "This came for you yesterday, and I was waiting for the right moment to give it to you."

He smiled and accepted the book, running his fingers over the gold lettering.

"How does it feel?" I questioned.

"Amazing. It feels like we have come full circle, you know?"

"I do know, and if you have anything planned for after *The Raven Returns*, I think this would be a great place to start."

He remained silent when I handed him a wrapped box. He slowly peeled back the paper and the ribbon, and inside was a silver frame with an ultrasound photo of our baby. He studied the picture, and I saw droplets of tears fall over the glass. I knew I was the weepy one in our relationship who can cry at the drop of a dime, but to see Seamus do it…broke my heart in some way. He never held back with his feelings, especially with me.

When he finally looked up at me from the framed photo, he looked already like a father in love with his child. He said nothing but placed the frame down and put his hands on my flat stomach.

"Our child. We're having a baby," he said, his endearing words were beyond expressive.

I put my hands over his and said yes. In less than a second, I was on my back with Seamus over me. He kissed me all over as if I was his last meal. We were out in the open where anyone could see, and for the first time I was feeling a little bashful for being so exposed.

I didn't have a spot on my body that didn't have his mark on it. His eyes never left mine as he slowly began to make love to me. We connected in all ways possible, and soon we would be parents.

"I love you, Shaena. You will never know how deep my love is for you, and now you are carrying our child. You have made me so happy."

As I rocked our newborn son, Brendan Colin Maxwell O'Toole, I silently laughed to myself. He certainly had a long name, but how could I not include our beloved fathers for our first son?

I remember how Seamus gave me a book on baby names, and we sat up one night to make a list of our favorites. I knew immediately what I wanted as soon as I read the meaning behind the name. Seamus loved it too and agreed choosing this name was symbolic to our history. Brendan means "little raven," and it fit him so perfectly with his dark head of hair that matched mine.

Brendan had fallen fast asleep as I finished nursing him. His little cheek was nestled against my chest. Our little boy looked quite content with a full belly of milk.

I looked down to our son sleeping soundly when I heard a clicking sound.

"I'm sorry, love. I had to capture this moment. Your beauty is a work of art, holding our son like a renaissance painting. You see? Look at it, my love."

"I love how you see me. You were the only one that ever did. Thank you for crashing into me."

"Thank you for trusting that I would catch you from the spectator stands."

"Thank you for making me a wife and a mother."

"Thank you for making me a husband and a father."

"You know love, we could do this all day, and I would never tire of telling you how much I love you, and now that love is extended to our son."

After I placed Brendan down in his nursery, Seamus asked me to take a walk with him down to the newly constructed greenhouse he had built on the grounds. The warm and well-lit house was vast and filled with wall-to-wall flowers consisting of violets, hibiscus, lilies, orchids, and my favorite, roses. He held my hand throughout the short walk from our home to the greenhouse. I knew our son was safe with Aideen's sister as our nanny, but after only a few minutes away from him, I already missed Brendan terribly. Seamus could notice my apprehension and pulled me closer as we reached the house. I sat down on a bench and warmed my hands.

"Are you warmer now, love?"

My cheeks began to flush as he cupped my face. He was such an attentive lover, never missing anything when it came to pleasing me. He clipped a single stemmed purple rose from the growing pot, and after removing the thorns, held it in his hand.

"Happy anniversary, my love," he said as he knelt down before me and held the blossoming flower.

"Anniversary? Did I miss something?" I nervously questioned.

"No worries, I'll be happy to remind you. This time last year, I handed you a purple rose and implored you to remember who was standing before you: not the famous writer, but the man who never stopped loving you. Your eyes were bright but guarded until the memories came flooding back to you. You knew but were scared to say the words aloud in fear they may not be true. Do remember the memory I shared with you on that day?"

"Yes. You reminded me of the time I first questioned you to why you always give me purple roses."

"And what did I say?"

"You said, 'Don't you know? I give you the purple rose because it represents love at first sight, a love I have felt from the first moment my eyes found yours, or better yet, when your body crashed into mine.'"

"Exactly, and now a year later, here we are."

He kissed me passionately, stood up and walked over to a basket of flowers. It was a bouquet of dark pink, coral, white, and one blue rose. They were gorgeous and wrapped in delicate lace and ribbons. I recognized the material immediately. It was extra material left over from my wedding dress. Now I knew why Seamus was so intent on saving it after I found it in a box a few months back. He knew what he wanted to do with it, and he saved it for this moment here with me.

"For you, Shaena. You already know what the purple rose represents, allow me to share the rest with you. The dark pink represents my gratitude for making me all that I am. My greatest role in this life is your lover, husband, and father to our child. The coral one is for desire, and it is to show you how I so easily lose myself into you when I look at you. The white one will serve as a reminder for me to always be worthy of your love, as you are of mine. You doubted it once before, and it nearly broke me. I will always prove to you how cherished you are to me. Finally, the blue one. It means the impossible. Once upon a time, we were so unattainable that we stopped believing, but you saying the words to me a year ago broke that theory and made it a reality.

It was the beginning of our new life together."

He handed me the bouquet and kissed me, whispering how much he loved and will always love me. As we walked hand-in-hand back up to the house, I felt lighter, as if I was floating and high on Seamus.

Leaping into the arms of the boy with curly red hair and freckles was the best decision I ever made in my life. He was easy to trust and made me believe that if I took that leap of courage with him, he would always catch me.

Thank god I did, because I have been falling ever since.

BONUS SCENE

War Room...Part Two

Jesse

"**O**kay, people, listen up. Shaena will be here any minute with a signed contract in hand from Weston James. Today our company competes with the world. Today we become global, and it is just the beginning."

"Gee, James, tell us how you really feel."

He stopped abruptly to address my interruption. All eyes were on us. The sexual tension between us was strong, and it would not be contained for much longer. One thing you do not do on War Room day is interrupt the boss, but we were so much more than that, and it was becoming clear to everyone in the room.

"Something to say, Jesse?" he asked calmly but with an underlying curt tone.

"I have plenty to say, James, but I'm just not too sure you want me to say it in front of an audience."

I knew taunting him was not the smartest thing I could do, especially with Shae due here soon, but he deserved it after giving me the cold shoulder and confusing signals. Did he want me or not? When we were in bed, I clearly knew his intentions, but to the rest of the world, he treated me like I was just another guy in the crowd. Well, fuck that, not today. James was going to see me, and if it was our last time together, then he was definitely going to remember my parting gift.

His angry eyes never left mine as I knew he was about to have everyone clear the room. What was about to happen did not require an audience.

"That's a wrap, people. You have your fuel, so now go out there and light some fires. You smell it…sell it."

Everyone left the room, thinking that I was about to get my ass handed to me. Who was he kidding? That sexy fucker. I was up for playing his game.

He swallowed deeply, showing me his neck muscles. I loved running my tongue over his Adam's apple every time we fucked. He could not get enough of the sensation he felt when I did it. Was he thinking about it now? His neck was bitable and so inviting for me to sink my teeth into now, but I had other ideas where I wanted to place my mouth.

After the last person walked out and closed the door behind him, James turned to me and said, "Okay Jesse, the floor is yours. What's gotten you so hot and bothered?"

Oh yeah, just the reaction I was looking for! He wasn't pissed; he was turned on. Talk about lighting some fires, that's all I wanted to do when I looked at him. His cool exterior could scare the shit out of everyone who worked for him, but for me, it turned me on as I had never felt before.

He stood tall in his six foot three long and lean frame. I knew what he looked like underneath his designer suits and how his body felt against mine when he shared my bed with me. He wanted me, this I knew.

He never shifted his eyes, as I got closer to him. His arms crossed with a determined expression as I was now standing in front of him. This was the game we played with each other: push and pull until one of us breaks, but I was taking the wheel today.

James was clearly the dominant in our relationship. He only allowed me so much room to play, and then he would regain his composure and take back his control. Time to show James whom he belonged to and end this bullshit for the last time.

I could feel his breath on my lips, and if I were to touch his tenting dick, I would feel the pre-come leaking from his slit. I reached for his neck and pulled him closer, where I crushed my mouth on his and forced him to open for me. Our tongues did this vicious dance for dominance. He moaned in pleasure, unzipped, and there it was—Boom!— the green light for me to take what I wanted and craved like my next meal.

I held James in place with him panting between moans and breaths. He wanted me just as much as I wanted him, but he kept holding back time and time again. What was he afraid of? The door was not locked, and I knew we could be interrupted at any moment, but I had to take my chance and force him to see what we could have if he would just allow himself to.

He held my gaze, and then his strong hands gripped my shoulders to lower me down to my knees. He gave me just enough access to take what I wanted. His delicious cock disappeared down my throat as he held me in place.

I took him as deep as I could without choking, and as his balls tightened, I knew he was close to exploding. I would drink every drop he spilled into my mouth and always crave more.

"I'm close, Jesse, so fucking close."

I gripped his bare ass and dug my fingers into his flesh. Like hell, was I releasing him? Gripping my hair, James exploded all he had down my throat. With the last of his hot seed swallowed, I gave him what he needed to see: a look of pure satisfaction. This was for him. I could take care of myself later, but I had a feeling I would not have to do it alone.

Something shifted when he looked down to meet my eyes staring back up at him. There was no more denying what I had known from the first moment we shared a bed: James was mine, and I was his.

His strong arms pulled me up by my shoulders and held me close to his body. Our dicks were rubbing up against each other like a cock-fight for dominance. I wanted him so badly, and I was a step away from clearing his desk so he could take me, until we were interrupted.

My phone vibrated from my pocket. Shaena was in the building and making her way upstairs. Perfect timing.

I wiped the corners of my mouth and looked back over to James. No words were spoken, just a look to be continued, and in private.

When he finally let out a breath, he released me. Always the polished one. He looked all put back together, never giving away anything as to what just happened here. I was okay with that, for now.

ACKNOWLEDGMENTS

Thank you to my close-knit circle who make up "Team Sparkle." My accomplishments would not be complete without the very talented professionals who help me make my work come to life.

Every book idea begins with my editor, Joe Marron. He gives me that little push that I sometimes need to delve deeper into my characters and develop the *extra* that I need to make my story great. Your encouragement keeps me going at times when I get frustrated, although your red pen continues to scare me. LOL! It's all good, my friend.

When the book is edited and read a hundred times, the next step is formatting. The very talented Julie Titus of JT Formatting takes over and creates a beautiful interior that sets the tone for the words you will read.

For Alice Tribue, you are a godsend when it comes to blurb writing. Thank you my friend.

I try to be as unique as possible when it comes to designing my book covers. I also try to choose a photo that relates to my story. Once again, I have found the perfect one and had the very talented and creative Sara Eirew design the cover for *Return to Kildare*. Thank you, my friend. I love it!

Thank you to my family and friends for your love and support. I could not do this without you.

Lastly, Team Sparkle would not be complete without giving thanks to some very special friends who share my work and cheer me on. Thank you from my heart!

Nancy Gennes Metsch
Florence Richards
Aideen McGann
Karen Bennett
Mindy Guerreiros
Angela Seattle

ABOUT THE AUTHOR

Mary A. Wasowski is a Best Selling Author who writes adult contemporary romance. Best known for her *Forever Series*, this is her seventh publication.

A romantic at heart, she is an avid reader when she's not writing. Her Kindle goes everywhere with her! Born and raised in New Jersey, she shares her life with her husband, Henry, and their three sons. She now lives in North Carolina and works as a full-time writer.

I would love to hear from you.
Please stay connected wherever you are.

EMAIL:
AuthorMaryAWasowski@gmail.com

FACEBOOK:
https://www.facebook.com/pages/Author-Mary-A-Wasowski

TWITTER:
https://twitter.com/wasow6

MARY A. WASOWSKI

INSTAGRAM:
https://instagram.com/authormaryawasowski/

WEBSITE:
http://authormaryawasowski.com/

GOODREADS:
https://www.goodreads.com/author/show/6949510.Mary_A_Wasowski

GOOGLE +:
https://plus.google.com/+MaryWasowski

TSU:
http://www.tsu.co/authormaryawasowski

OTHER BOOKS

by Mary A. Wasowski

A Changed Life (standalone)

Forever Series:

Forever: Book One
Second Chance at Forever: Book Two
Our Forever Promise: Book Three

All Roads Lead Home (standalone)
An Unfinished Life (standalone)

www.ingramcontent.com/pod-product-compliance
Lightning Source LLC
Chambersburg PA
CBHW071251250626
47163CB00002B/414